LIMBO

LIMBO

---

by
JACQUELINE HONNET

For Stan & Sandy.

*Hope you enjoy these
stories.*

Jacqueline

TURNSTONE PRESS

Limbo
copyright © Jacqueline Honnet 2005

Turnstone Press
Artspace Building
607-100 Arthur Street
Winnipeg, MB
R3B 1H3 Canada
www.TurnstonePress.com

Turnstone Press gratefully acknowledges the assistance of The Canada Council for the Arts, the Manitoba Arts Council, the Government of Canada through the Book Publishing Industry Development Program and the Government of Manitoba through the Department of Culture, Heritage and Tourism, Arts Branch, for our publishing activities.

Canada Council for the Arts   Conseil des Arts du Canada

MANITOBA CONSEIL DES arts COUNCIL DU MANITOBA

Canadä

Cover design: Doowah Design
Interior design: Sharon Caseburg
Printed and bound in Canada by Friesens for Turnstone Press.

Library and Archives Canada Cataloguing in Publication

Honnet, Jacqueline, 1972-
Limbo / Jacqueline Honnet.

ISBN 0-88801-310-8

1. Women—Fiction. I. Title.

PS8615.O53L54 2005   C813'.6   C2005-904054-8

For David and Clarissa Honnet, my wonderful parents

Contents

LIMBO

FUNERAL STORIES

MY HUSBAND TELLS ME ANOTHER FUNERAL STORY. THE TIME HE IS five and goes to Estevan for his uncle's funeral.

"I didn't know my uncle was a twin," he says. "And as we move into the pew, his brother—my dead uncle—walks through the chapel door. I thought maybe he was *supposed* to attend, and when it was time, he'd climb into the coffin, close the lid and they'd carry him away."

I pile my dinner plate on top of my husband's. "Then what happened?" I ask, motioning to him across the counter with a fork.

"At the gravesite I realize something is wrong," he laughs. "They are lowering the coffin into the ground and I want to shout, *Run, Run*, before someone notices he isn't inside."

I plug the teakettle in and settle back in my chair. "That's twelve," I say. "Between us, we've been to twelve funerals."

My first funeral is hot. It's a sticky August morning and I am seven. My father comes to wake me. I hear the *clap, clap* of my mother closing kitchen cupboards. He kneels beside me, holding his head in his hands, and my half-asleep mind thinks that maybe I am in trouble. For what? I'm not sure. I stare at him, trying to figure out his expression, until finally he says, "Grandpa is gone."

I sit up in bed and wrap my arms tightly around his neck. I'm not sure what he means by *gone*, and I'm also not certain why I am hugging him. But I'm relieved when he hugs me back.

For the next three days, my mother mumbles into the phone, writes endless notes on a thick pad of yellow paper, and leaves the house with a blue scarf tied loosely around her head. My father cooks. But not pork chops and rice or spicy chicken, mostly burnt eggs and toast. The nights my mother is out, he lets my sister and me play Chinese Checkers until nine o'clock and never reminds me to brush my teeth. My mother and her sisters are out shopping through racks of suits and dress shirts, picking out clothes for my grandpa—who never owned a suit— to meet God. In bed at night, I wonder if they had to take him along to try on clothes and, if so, who carried his big body into the change room?

At the funeral, broad hips pen me in and tissue-filled hands direct me into place. Dark suit jackets and black dresses create an opaque wall, blocking air and light. I can hardly see my grandpa, but from where I stand he looks like he's napping in his recliner. Women flutter hymnals, moving stale air around and around. I rest my face against my mother's hand and am surprised by her cold skin in the warm heat. She looks straight ahead and doesn't tell me to stop when I pull my dress up, hoping to catch a breeze. I tuck the front into my panties, look proudly down at the patent leather shoes my father bought me especially for the funeral. I wonder if he picked them out by himself and if there is a special store for funeral shoes—ones that are good for standing and kneeling, and don't look like party shoes. I wonder if they are the same kind they bury little girls in. And if I'd get a new dress with a lacy collar and gloves to match if one of my parents died.

I am lying in bed when my husband says, "What would you do if I died?" He rolls away, takes off his glasses and places them on the nightstand. "Are you listening?" he asks, propping himself up on a pillow.

I knit my eyebrows and look over the top of my book. "I'm listening," I sigh, "how do you die?"

"What do you mean, *how do I die?*"

"You said, *what would I do if you died?* How do you die in this scenario?"

"Does it matter?"

"Yes, it matters. Are you ill for a long time, or is it sudden, like an accident?" I place my open book on my chest and hold his face playfully between my hands. "Are we talking long-term suffering, or just shock?"

"Okay, maybe a car accident, or a mountain-climbing fall," he says.

"But you don't climb." I smooth his forehead, as if checking for a fever.

"Maybe *that's* why I have the accident," he says, laughing.

"I'd cry a little and then I'd bury you." I smile. "Now stop, I'm reading." I flip onto my stomach and hold my head up with one hand.

My husband smoothes the cool white sheet over the back of my thighs. "You wouldn't have to work anymore," he says matter-of-factly. "At least not for a long time."

"Great," I say, glancing at him, "that's a comfort."

Before we were married, he was more likely to talk about his favourite part of the day (the moment he hears the clatter of my keys in his door) or his favourite part of my body (my baby toes), and now I wonder if this is what my girlfriend meant when she said, "Once you're married, even the sound of his voice won't be the same."

Now he asks me questions like: Buried or cremated? Church or funeral chapel? Beloved wife or beloved wife and daughter?

"If I go first, you should just cremate me and dump me in the Bow," he says confidently. "I mean, unless you want a gravesite to visit."

"The Bow River? Is that legal?" I ask, closing the book.

"Why not? Here's what you do, put me in a tin can, or something equally innocuous, and toss me out your window as you drive the 4th Street fly-over."

"Oh, that sounds lovely, we'll take your brother's van so the whole family can do it together," I say, laughing. "Unfortunately," I say, settling my head on his chest, "you will rot in the ground under a modest, yet touching, headstone, just like the rest of our Catholic families."

I recently ordered legal will kits over the Internet; before they arrived my husband took to saying "Drive *really* carefully," as I left for work each morning. I suppose he was actually more worried about me than the $10,000 life insurance policy my parents started for me in high school. But at the time I was angry and stuffed the blank pages under a stack of unopened pantyhose in my dresser drawer. I finally fill out the forms the night he singes his eyebrows trying to fix the toaster. I see the flash out the corner of my eye and when I reach him he looks like my uncle, who had cancer. He just laughs, takes me in his arms, saying, "*That* was a close one."

My husband and I meet friends for dinner at my favourite Greek restaurant. It's the week after they roll their Honda on the way to Banff. We meet them in the parking lot; my girl-friend has her left arm in a white cotton sling and asks me to fix her hair.

"It was late that night and I was so tired," she says. "I

thought—if I just close my eyes for a second. And then boom—thank God the baby wasn't with us."

I gently clip the tortoiseshell barrette in her shiny black hair and put my arm around her as we walk into the restaurant. They seat us at a tiny table beside the window, filled with votive candles and a deep basket of warm pita bread and hummus. I am spreading my napkin in my lap when she puts a picture of the wreckage on my dinner plate. My husband says, "Holy shit." I want to move the picture off the plate. I pour myself another glass of water and listen to my husband say words like *lucky* and *grateful*, and am surprised he doesn't call the accident *a close one.*

We all sip red wine and discuss their insurance claim. My husband asks if there's a passenger-side airbag in the new Jetta they plan to buy next month. I want to lighten the mood. "What colour?" I ask, then wish I hadn't, stuffing my mouth with pita bread. By the time the entrées arrive they've moved on to *crumple zones* and *side-impact beams.*

I have just taken a mouthful of eggplant moussaka when my girlfriend falls silent and glances anxiously at her husband. She inhales sharply, then asks if we would become legal guardians for their baby girl, if they died. My husband says, "Wow," and I blink at him, trying to figure out if he means yes or no. I smile out of reflex and push the word *maybe* from my tight throat as I rest my hand on top of hers. It didn't occur to me that every time I've scooped their daughter into my arms, they were imagining I was thinking *maybe soon* about having my own baby instead of just *maybe.* On the way to the car we make plans for coffee, agree this is a big decision and promise to give it some thought.

At home, I listen to my husband brushing his teeth as I lie in bed. He walks up and down in front of the mirror, and pulls his toothbrush from his foamy mouth to ask questions like: Won't their families be angry they asked *us?* Where would she sleep? Would she call you Mommy? Could we change her name?

I had thought myself generous, offering to babysit when she was smaller, and even secretly wished she were mine as her tiny body generated such heat against my chest. It has been months, though, since I've seen her and I imagine she won't be so easy to lift, her body will press heavily on my shoulder. My husband says, "Let's sleep on it," as he turns off the light and walks over to the bedroom window. He pulls the blinds up and a blue glow washes the room. In this light he looks thinner than usual, and his skin is paler than ever. I pull my knees to my chest and cross my arms tightly around them.

I am twelve when my neighbour is murdered by her husband. My sister and I are swinging high above the fence on our yellow and white swing set when we hear the bang. My outstretched legs seem to float over the top of our neighbour's roof; my toes skim the soft grass as I bend my knees to lift myself higher. The noise is like a pop, leaving us both motionless. I tell my sister it's a car backfiring, the way my mother does when I flinch at loud noises. I am in bed that night when my mother, on the phone, says, "My God. A gun."

For what seems like hours, my father sits on the floor between my and my sister's single beds, holding our hands and whispering, "Hush. Sleep now." Through the open window, I hear back gates slamming as neighbours gather in the back alley to console and update one another. I want to ask my father if the police will come around to ask questions. To see if anyone saw anything. Heard anything. I picture myself in an interrogation room with my sister, sipping Coke and promising to tell the whole truth, nothing but. My father eventually drops my sweaty hand, rubs his face. He leans against my bed and I think maybe I should offer to sleep in my sister's so he can have mine. But my throat feels tight and my tongue too big to talk. I turn towards the wall and slip the bottom of my face under the covers. My hot breath feels suffocating and I wonder if my sister is sleeping or thinking about the *pop*.

I am washing a sink full of dishes when I tell my husband the story. "My mother didn't take us to that funeral," I say.

For nights that summer I lay awake, trying to picture my neighbour's slender face shouting, "Hello girls," over the back fence. When it finally came into focus, it was detached from her body, bobbing like a yo-yo. Months later a new family moved into the house. I can still remember walking with my mother as she carried a yellow cake to their front door. I tell my husband how I didn't want to step inside, but she pushed, gently. The new neighbour called me a lovely young lady, but I still sat closer to my mother than usual. My mother drank her tea in too-big gulps from her white porcelain cup as the new neighbour talked about her *discomfort* with the history of the house.

"I had to pee so badly," I tell my husband. "But I was too afraid to walk down the hall and find bloodstains on the carpet."

"Did you really see blood?" my husband asks with wide eyes.

"I was twelve years old and frightened," I say. "Anything would have looked like blood to me." I turn and squirt Sunlight into the metal roasting pan.

"Why did he shoot her?" he asks.

"I'm not sure, something about her not wanting to move back east."

"He shot her for that?"

"Some days I'd shoot you for less," I say, smiling.

"But seriously, could you ever imagine being that mad at me?" he asks, kissing the back of my neck.

"Yes, I don't have to imagine."

I add more hot water to the sink as he says, "You wouldn't ever *really* hurt me, would you?" I roll my eyes. "Let me finish those dishes, okay?" he says. "You take it easy."

"My grandpa's funeral had great food," my husband tells me. He is sitting at the dining-room table, looking at the family tree his grandmother gave him for safekeeping on her last visit. "It was like a bake-off. All his sisters came with at least two dishes. Peach cobbler, shortbread, cheese biscuits," he says, pointing to the cooks on the chart. "Potato salad and cold fried chicken. Us kids took a whole cake behind the church hall. No one even noticed."

"What kind?" I ask.

"Orange pound cake," he says, scanning the family tree for a corresponding name. "There she is. The kind with the bits of grated orange rind in it."

I move his finger so I can read the name of the orange pound cake baker. "You're lucky," I say, "our funerals mostly had pre-made finger sandwiches, vegetable trays from Safeway." I pull the chart in front of me and trace my finger over his grandparents and parents. "You're the end of the line," I say, pointing to the empty space beneath his name. I flip to the back of the sheet that lists dates of birth, marriage, death and burial.

"I should get that pound cake recipe," my husband says, smacking his hand down on the table. "You know, now, before they're all gone."

My husband and I have a dinner party. When the last guest finally leaves, he grabs me round the waist and says, "Bed-time." But I can't sleep with the dishes piled high on the counter and rings of red wine on the linen tablecloth. I collect dirty glasses from the living room and stuff unused napkins in the wicker basket beside the fridge. I kneel on the edge of the living room carpet and pick peanuts from the coarse straw area rug. I toss a second handful on the coffee table and decide to leave it for now, to shake it out in the morning. I go upstairs, undress and wash my face in the darkened bathroom.

"Who would take our kid if we died?" my husband says, a dim shadow sitting up in bed.

"We don't have a kid."

"I know, but what if we did?"

"I don't know," I say in an exasperated tone.

"Is it like weddings, do you have to ask the people who asked you to take care of theirs?" He gets up and pulls me into bed on top of him. "Do you know who my parents were going to leave my brothers and me to? My fat auntie." I laugh and roll off him. "She had loose skin around her arms," he says. "And this yucky baby powder paste between the folds of her neck. She called me *Sport*, and slipped beef jerky into my pocket whenever we visited."

I close my eyes and listen to my husband tell me one more story. How his grandmother's first four baby boys died before they reached their first birthdays. How with each birth she carefully inscribed the certificate with the exact same name, and even after the third death she refused to believe that a word contained the power to take another baby. All four were buried in a row in a tiny Saskatchewan graveyard, just off the highway, each headstone an exact replica of the one beside it, except for the year. My husband says, "My father ran away at fifteen to escape his miserable mother." But I imagine it was the weight of his name that was too heavy to bear. "Maybe we should take their baby girl now," my husband whispers. "What if none of ours survive?"

"I figured out when we're going to die," my husband shouts from the study as I walk in the front door.

I set the grocery bags on the kitchen table and say, "Well, as long as it's not in the next five minutes, could you please help unpack these groceries?"

"June 17, 2052, for you and September 30, 2045, for me," he says, grabbing two cans of pineapple chunks.

"And how did you figure this out, oh clairvoyant one?" I hang my jacket on the front hook and look over the grocery receipt.

"It's this great Web site," he says. "You just answer twenty questions and bingo."

"Eighty-five seems high, doesn't it?" I say absentmindedly, sticking the receipt on the corkboard.

"2052," he says. "That makes you eighty-two, not eighty-five."

"Enough with the death wishes, I was talking about the food bill."

"These will take years off you," he says, waving a box of oatmeal cookies at me.

"Stop it," I say, grabbing the box. "You're creeping me out. Besides, don't you think you should ask someone before you determine her death date? What if I didn't want to know?"

"Who wouldn't want to know?" he says. "Now we have a time frame to work with, and I figure maybe having kids isn't such a good idea—that's a lot of time we could be travelling alone." He pulls me towards him and kisses me on the nose. "If I lose ten pounds or you start smoking, we could die the same year."

"What?" I push away from him.

"I just thought it would be nice if we died the same year."

"Who says I don't want you to die first?" I say. "Maybe I have other plans."

"To get remarried? You'll be like seventy-five, for God-sakes." He shakes his head.

"And you'll be dead, so I can do whatever I want."

"Throw me the cookies, grumpy," he says, holding his hands out in front of him. "If you're going to be like that I won't show you the nice obituary I generated for you on the Web site."

My husband and I are still in bed when my mother calls to say my favourite great-aunt has died. I lower the receiver into my lap and her words become mumbles. I am reluctant to hold the phone close. I don't want to hear the words that remove her from my life; I don't want to hear my mother say, "Everything will be all right," in her calm and stony voice.

"Should I come? I mean, I want to, if *you* want me to," my husband says as he watches me stuff pants and sweaters into a small blue suitcase.

"It's up to you," I say, not looking up. "You only met her a few times." I continue packing, but am relieved when he tosses his black toiletries bag on the bed. He holds my hand during the entire trip, stopping only to put my bag in the overhead compartment.

I am in my aunt's bedroom when I hold up a tattered blue dress and say, "This was her favourite."

The neckband is coming apart where she'd tug the collar out over the neck of her beige cardigan, smoothing her hands down her sides and saying, "Ready as I'll ever be." I remove a brooch from the collar, just as I have from her embroidered cream blouse and a dark blue jumper. I place the brooch with the others in a crystal jar on her water-stained nightstand, and stare at the small ceramic dish containing her teeth. She had no children and my family has not decided if they want a viewing. I wonder if the funeral home will need the teeth, so I slip a handkerchief over them, just as she slipped her hand over her sunken mouth and mumbled, "Goodnight dear," each time I visited.

Her bedroom reminds my husband of vacations with his parents: a lumpy motel bed with a cheap cotton spread and matching curtains, a small TV on the dressing table in the corner. Times when the only decision he had to make was whether to get a grilled cheese sandwich from room service or eat at the diner across the street. My husband plunks himself down on the thin mattress and liberates a halo of dust. The room's stale cracker odour has a sobering effect. I unfold my aunt's ivory handkerchief, holding the red and gold brooch I have decided to keep as a memento.

"They called a few days ago about the baby," I say, not looking at my husband.

"They did?"

"I didn't tell you because we haven't decided yet."

"What will we tell her?" my husband asks.

I grip the brooch. "I guess we'll say we just don't feel comfortable—"

"No, what will we tell the baby about what happened to them?"

"I suppose that depends on what happens—maybe everything will be fine and we won't have to tell her anything."

"Yeah, but just in case, we should think of a story."

How to Raise a Smart Baby

I HAVE ALWAYS BEEN AFRAID OF FROGS. MY MOTHER LOVES TO TELL the story. "Do you remember the frog?" she says. No matter how many times I say *yes*, she retells it. I roll my eyes as she embellishes the size (it was not as big as her fist) and the intensity of my scream (at six I could not possibly have sounded like a foghorn). My mother is not usually one for silly stories, she delights in the practical: that by five I could run my own bath, that I didn't pick off one chicken-pox scab, that I was a clever baby who walked at eight months and never needed a pacifier. She laughs, "You and that damn frog."

The frog jumps out of the tub faucet. First, I turn the tap and no water comes out. The rainwater on the island is collected in a cistern—a pool, I learn, for tadpoles and other horrible creatures. When the bathroom taps shudder open, out streams a tiny frog in rotten-egg-smelling water. I scream, hop out of the tub, convinced that frog legs, not air, skim the tiny hairs on my body. I squeeze my eyes shut, put both hands between my legs. This is how I am standing, barely peeking through eye slits, when my mother's face fills the doorway.

My mother can kill anything, I tell my friends at school. This is my proud picture of her, someone who murders small beasts that invade our home. She has a certain look as she moves through the house, fly swatter or tightly rolled newspaper in hand. Eyes traced with black liquid eyeliner and a dishtowel tucked in her waistband. Prettier than most mothers. Meaner still. She always grabs me in a way that I first mistake for a hug, then moves me out of the way. "Stop crying, it's practically over," she says. Centipedes make their way up to the ceiling, where she delivers the swift and lethal blow with the end of a broom handle. She is fast, and she is right. The centipedes never have a chance.

She doesn't kill the frog. She shoos it out the back door. Slams it hard. I am embarrassed by the way I scream. The pitiful way I curl up onto the kitchen chair. My mother stands me up, pats my back with a round of quick taps. I imagine she is eager to get back to her cooking, but remembers to say, "You're fine. There, now." I don't stop my warm sniffling against her leg, though. I hold on as long as I can, while she continues chopping thick tomato wedges with a meat cleaver, tossing them into a silver bowl that clangs against the counter.

———

Today my mother is chopping onions for biryani. Her latest project is East Indian cooking. Last year was aerobics, when she bought cherry red tights and a black sleeveless tank top with the words GO FOR IT scrawled across the chest in neon pink. Cardio Funk, Kick Start, Power Cycle, Boxercize, Step Pump. She calls me often to describe a challenging footstep and remind me, "It's not too late to start—you're a quick learner, like me." But she quits the classes within six months, saying, "Those instructors are complete amateurs." She buys her own step and workout videos—sets up a mini-gym in her basement.

She gives me a workout tape for Christmas, which my roommate watches over and over, trying to figure out if the purple-clad workout woman was the valedictorian of her high school. "That's what happens when you're too smart for your own good," she shouts at the TV.

I am standing at my sink, scrubbing the waxy skins of red and green peppers for the biryani. My mother hums a peppy tune. I can't make it out, the sound warped by the hunk of doughy bread she insists on sucking. "It stops onion tears," she says with authority as she stuffs a ball of my $4.99-a-loaf organic flaxseed bread into her mouth. I like chopping onions—the things it lets me cry about: the grapefruit-sized ovarian cyst I had at sixteen that may have rendered me sterile; the plaid-shirt guy in my physics class whom I should have asked for help, putting me on the road to medical school instead of marketing, the old boyfriend I could be married to, living in Springbank, instead of sharing a condo with a roommate in Dalhousie.

"Damn onions," I say, half smiling.

I scrape the onions into the wide pan my mother says makes all the difference. I stir them with a wooden spoon. "Like this," my mother says, bumping me to the side with her hip. "Stir like this."

"Where do you keep all your useless information?" I say, running my hand through her curls.

"I just love learning," she says, tapping the side of her head for emphasis. *Thump, thump.* I picture her head as a big drum, her face stretched across the opening like cowhide, pieces of information echoing from cheek to forehead, temple to chin: *Tips for Aging Beauty, Growing Giant Ferns, Mastering Culinary Delights, Aloe: Its Many Uses, How to Raise a Smart Baby.*

———

When I move to Canada at seven I think there has been some kind of mistake. My mother tells me it will be sunny. I stand shivering, my back pressed against the chain-linked fence in the schoolyard, watching other children in shirtsleeves and short pants. How was I supposed to know that *sunny* doesn't always mean hot? It seems to me that the sun shouldn't be allowed to shine in such cold. They assigned me a buddy, a girl with a blue-jean pencil case with little back pockets to hold paperclips and erasers, a girl who likes to raise her hand every time the teacher asks a question, a girl who probably asked to be my buddy because she thinks she knows everything. I manage to slip away from her when the bell rings, and now, outside, I change my mind and look around at faces, trying to find hers, hoping nobody asks me another stupid question. What do they eat in the Bahamas? Have you ever seen a hurricane? Did you have school on the beach? Do you speak the same kind of English there? What's wrong with you? Why aren't you answering my questions?

———

I take my mother's advice about learning and sign up for art at the university. Thursday nights, I do hurried sketches of naked volunteers. My instructor starts us out with short poses, models changing position every ten seconds, but now we have graduated to longer poses of forty-five minutes. I knew the models would be naked, the course description said so, but I am still surprised by how unceremoniously they sit, crouch, or stand, leaning on a chair as though in their own kitchen, fixing a late-night sandwich. The male model wears a dull terry towel bathrobe with a frayed belt and a hole in the armpit. I imagine it's the same robe he watches morning TV in while waiting for coffee to brew, the one he spit toothpaste foam on—causing the terry cloth to form a rough, spiky patch that will stay until he washes it. I admire the ease with which he exposes himself. I have only been naked in front of three people, and then not at the same time. Locker room showers and being a child don't count. I never like the feeling. My exposed body stiffening like plaster under inspection.

———

A picture of myself at seven. The back reads: *Schooldays, 1979.* In the photograph it is the week before we move. My dark eyes bulge with excitement. I am in my school uniform, brown and white check with a round collar, standing on a small stretch of sand, the glint of water in the background. My last day of school, arms laden with going-away gifts: a gold St. Christopher pin, a folding map of the Bahamas (a blue *x* marking the site of my schoolyard), a straw bag with my name embroidered in salmon pink on the front flap. I am surprised when my mother asks if there is something special I want to do before leaving the island. I imagine now she meant: get a spicy meat patty from the gas station, go to Paradise Island for a last swim, buy a bunch of juicy guineps from the fruit stand on Bluehill Road. I ask her to drive me from one end of the island to the other. Start at the gates of Lyford Cay and drive all the way to Yamacraw. And she does. She takes the picture out east, on a beach far from home, where we picnic and my mother quizzes me on the names of Canadian provinces. And I keep forgetting Prince Edward Island. My mother doesn't remember any of this. She says my father took the picture in Goodman's Bay across the road from our house.

———

A bulletin board at the university reads: IQ TESTS, VOLUNTEERS REQUIRED—SIGN UP TODAY. I think maybe I will. That I shouldn't take my brain for granted. I buy a book, *Brain Teasers*, to exercise my mental muscle. I read there is a marked decline in IQ with age—*once development is over it's not long before the process of aging starts pruning our brain cells, and the rate at which this happens may also be partly under our influence. This downslide starts as early as 30.* Maybe I can still age-proof my brain.

"You *are* smart," my mother says, not looking at me. "You don't need a test to tell you that."

I flip through the book and say, "Mum, it's for fun."

My mother used to take great delight in telling other people I was bright. She says, "I tell you she's gifted," to my newspaper-reading father in a too-loud voice when I bring home perfect spelling tests with words like *rectangle* and *scissors*. At seven it's the word *gifted* that strikes fear into me, although it is also funny the way it makes me think of Christmas and carefully wrapped boxes with shiny bows, instead of school. Gifted—the way you feel after all the presents are opened and you're sitting in the centre of crushed wrapping paper and silver curls of ribbon. No more surprises. Only now does it seem ironic that for me (the gifted one) the word needed so much explanation.

———

My roommate and I have started watching game shows—mostly *Jeopardy*! "IQ training," she says. I attempt to iron while she lies on the couch, wrapped in a grey throw blanket, eating the Smart Food popcorn she bought in honour of my upcoming test. She is convinced she can spot winners and losers the moment they step in front of the camera. "V-neck sweater and cords combo," she shouts. "Ladies and gentleman, we have a winner." I spray speed starch on the collars and shoulders of my shirts, the way my mother taught me, and press them during commercial breaks. "What is Avogadro's number, Alex?" my roommate shouts as I fish for more hangers in the bottom of the laundry basket. "Yes," she squeals, "cord boy is totally whipping their asses." I pull a pair of black dress pants out of the basket and wonder whether they're the right look for my test. "You should sit down and concentrate," my roommate says, "instead of pretending to iron. They are so going to ask you this kind of stuff on your IQ test."

I didn't see TV until I was seven. Reception on the island was bad, my mother tells me. "I don't have time to sit around," she says. I still feel like I'm indulging each time I watch, even when I'm ironing. My mother drags her ironing board outside in the drooping heat, sets it up on the patio. She puts the basket of clothes up on a table—safe from creatures. She says the humidity softens the wrinkles. Even when we move to this dry climate, she keeps the habit. Using the orange extension cord my father bought for the block heater, she prepares her pressing station. "Do you know that the sun gives us vitamin D?" she says. "This far north we need to increase our exposure."

———

I skip the second grade when I move. My mother insists. The school principal leads me into a meeting room on my first day.

"The psychologist will evaluate you," she says. "Your mother will wait in the hall." I sit in a rolling chair with blue cushions and black armrests. It does not seem the right type of chair for someone my size. I am shivering when the psychologist walks in, my dangling feet frozen with anticipation. The psychologist smells of cigarettes and vanilla as she brushes past me and settles into her chair.

"Some questions are designed to be difficult," she says. "If you cannot figure out the answer, simply say, 'I don't know,' and we'll move on." She sorts papers into piles, clanging her gold charm bracelet against the table with every movement. "Okay," she says. "Here's an example."

Which one of the following five is least like the other four?

THINK — SPEAK — WRITE — CALL — LISTEN

At home my mother explains to my father the difference between listening and hearing. "I am speaking," she says to my father, "but do you *hear* me?" I am listening and thinking, but the question doesn't make sense. I look down at my shoes, then at the psychologist. I grip my fingers on the edge of the table, and press sweaty circles onto the brown Formica. The fluorescent lights make my eyes water.

Which of the following five is least like the others?

CAT — FROG — LION — DOG — ELEPHANT

"Frog," I say so quickly I couldn't possibly have thought it through. Why? Because I hate frogs. Because they are heartless, crazed animals. "Because they just *aren't*—" I pause for her to say that I'm wrong.

"Warm-blooded? Is that what you were going to say—that they are not warm-blooded?"

"Yes," I say tentatively, surprised that I got the question right. I hear a scrape through the wall and imagine it's my mother scratching answers with her burgundy fingernails from her hallway seat. My toes are becoming numb and the ends of my words start rising into questions like balloons.

———

I am repotting plants. *Sole survivors*, I call them. There are only two plants left from the jungle my mother bought when I moved into my apartment. "Easy to care for," she assured me. I vowed to water them weekly, fertilize them monthly, put them closer to (or further away from) the window, according to the stiff plastic direction cards stuffed into the soil.

The bonsai tree is the first to go. "They always are," my roommate says wistfully. "Most people can't handle complicated." Most people with half a brain, I think, are cultivating whole vegetable patches, indoor herb gardens and even children. The people in the group home down the street sell enormous homegrown carrots and lettuce in their front yard every summer, which I eye enviously each time I pass.

I buy plant books in the discount bin at the Coles Books down the street. *Bonsai for Life*, one title reads, and I think it sounds like a good personal philosophy. I kill the bonsai within two weeks. It sits in my apartment for two more. At first I deny it is dead. I say things like, "It's just dry," or, "It's going through a dormant phase." I eventually throw it out, telling my mother it was a rare but deadly fungus. I keep the books on the coffee table, though, to prove to her I am a serious learner, that I know what I am doing.

The survivors are a variegated aurelia (that despite its fickle name has somehow managed to thrive) and a rubber tree (which everyone tells me is impossible to kill). They have outgrown their pots, roots bulging above the soil line, but I am reluctant to try anything different. I've had a simple plan so far. I water them when they look dry. And otherwise leave them alone. Afraid that too much care and attention may make them overly dependent. I drop the plant books in the blue charity bin at Safeway one Saturday, deciding I am an imposter, that *real* plant people will get better use out of them. I hate plant people. The ones who say, "I started it from a clipping," when I admire their hanging fern with the five-foot circumference. "It takes time," they reassure me. "Keep trying."

———

I edit brochure copy over diet Coke and Pringles at the kitchen table while my roommate pauses the game show tape she recorded for me. "Come sit down," she says. "That corporate crap is shrinking your brain."

The brochure is the kind I could write in my sleep, which is just as well since my mind has been drifting to IQ questions all week. *Our past success is the foundation upon which we build our future. We are committed inside and outside our organization, to: accountability, teamwork....* I read these brochures at work and they sound believable. Something about my office with its intercom, colour-coded filing system and seventeen-inch monitor adds credibility. *To continue to attract the brightest and the best, we must move forward. The time is now.* I get up and pull the blanket away from my roommate. "Fine, I'll just take a short break," I say, settling onto the couch.

"What's this," she says, clutching her hands dramatically to her chest. "No papers, no ironing board, no towel folding—ladies and gentlemen, can she sit still and watch TV?" She hits Play on the VCR and stuffs a handful of chips into her mouth.

———

... some say we are born with a specific level of intelligence that limits our potential for intellectual development. They argue that this intelligence quotient is governed by genetic factors, our IQ being largely determined by the interaction of our parents' genes. Broadly speaking, intelligent parents will produce intelligent children.

———

I eat an extra bowl of Sunny Boy with fresh blueberries and drink an extra cup of dark roast the morning of my IQ test. My roommate okays my navy sweater and grey pants, but before I walk out the door suggests black loafers instead of lace-ups.

I wait in a small classroom without windows. A young woman enters and introduces herself as the Master's student who will be conducting my test. I shift in my seat and wipe my sweaty hands down the front of my pants as she explains her career goals—the importance of practising the administration of the test. She reminds me that the results won't be available for five days, and tells me it is my choice whether or not to see them. "To your left is a one-way mirror where my classmates and instructor will be observing us," she says. I watch dim figures shuffle into chairs. They shut off the light behind the mirror and the Master's student tells me to pretend they are not looking. I raise my hand to wave hello, but instead tuck a piece of hair behind my ear. My stomach starts to churn and my hands tingle. I think about the workbook I should have read instead of watching *Jeopardy!*

After the test I walk home and think about a nature program I saw on TV. It said that if you drop a frog in boiling hot water, it'll jump out; but if you put it in warm water and slowly raise the temperature, the frog won't move and will eventually die.

I am smarter than a frog, I tell myself. I have the capacity to recognize an unhealthy situation.

––––––

Which of the following things will you never learn?

A) HOW TO MAKE PERFECT BLUEBERRY FLAN
B) HOW TO TYPE WITHOUT LOOKING AT YOUR KEYBOARD
C) HOW TO SOLVE MATH PROBLEMS INVOLVING POLAR COORDINATES
D) HOW TO DERIVE: $a + jb = re^{j\theta}$
E) WHAT 'IMAGINARY' NUMBERS HAVE TO DO WITH THE 'REAL' WORLD
F) THAT JUST BECAUSE TWO THINGS ARE RELATED DOESN'T MEAN THEY ARE THE SAME

––––––

"Like I was saying, your first IQ test was incorrect," my mother says casually as she whips egg whites with a professional whisk for a lemon meringue pie. She often talks like this, starting mid-thought, like someone has just asked her a question. Which I haven't. At first I think she means my score was abnormally high. I imagine, for a moment, she is trying to make me feel better, trying to lessen my disappointment in case these new test results are not as spectacular. IQ 145. The number my mother stuck on the kitchen fridge for the whole first term of grade three. The number that makes me feel sick when I bring home math sheets with simple equations marked wrong. "Practically a genius. Way above average," she says. "You just need to apply yourself."

"That stupid psychologist was wrong," she snorts now. "You are not average, 112 my foot."

"One hundred and twelve, not 145?" I shout after taking a gulp of hot coffee, scalding my tongue. "You lied, Mum?" My mother doesn't look at me, dumps the meringue on top of the pie.

"No, I did not lie. Do you hear me? That woman was wrong, you were just a nervous test taker," she says, creating impossibly high peaks in the topping.

———

She sat facing her mother, eyes glazed and unseeing, _____ and looking for a solution to this _____. All of her options in the given circumstances were exceedingly unpleasant.

A) COGITATING . . . DILEMMA

B) DREAMING . . . STALEMATE

C) PERUSING . . . PROBLEM

D) CONTEMPLATING . . . PUZZLE

E) I DON'T KNOW

———

I am wiping the phone down with paper towel and Windex, cleaning a small spot of salsa off the memory button. Lately, I've taken to listening to the dial tone. Sometimes it's a reassuring buzz—a sound that reminds me I could call. A buzz that could turn into a ring and a ring into a "Hello? It's me," followed by an "Oh, hello!" But other times it's a drone of nothingness. Like the way I used to press my ear to seashells when I was a girl. The harder I listen, the more the sound becomes a vibration that fills my head, my chest, my lungs, and I'm certain it somehow moves inside me. With each movement of my head the pitch changes and the reverberation intensifies or wanes.

"I'm listening to shell music," I shout to my mother as I kneel by the sea's foaming edge, conch shells mashed against both ears. She nods from beneath her shady bush, unpacking cold grapes and egg sandwiches from the tiny, white Styrofoam cooler. I think she understands, that she'd heard the music too, but as I press her number into the void of the dial tone I am certain my grape-peeling, crust-removing mother is ever only momentarily distracted.

———

Let's say that the following arguments are true:

    A) SOME GATEKEEPERS ARE WARRIORS.

    B) SOME WARRIORS ARE COWARDS.

Therefore, we can conclude that some gatekeepers must be cowards.

Is this conclusion TRUE *or* FALSE?

———

Sometimes things are true and false. I own a car (at least in fourteen more monthly payments of $422 I will), I own a condo (I painted the walls, ripped up the green carpeting and someday I will own more than eleven percent of the cozy dump), at work I am the least qualified (but strangely, the most prepared and the best paid).

Sometimes I dream I am awake. Sometimes I am awake when

I dream. When I am fully conscious I find myself saying, "I don't know. None of the above. Move on." I try to remember the questions for my answers. I wonder whether, in order to have the test scored, I need to have an answer for every question.

––––

Intelligence—a capacity for abstract thought; the ability to adapt to new situations; the capacity to learn or profit by experience; tautologically, the ability to do well in intelligence tests.

––––

"You are smarter than you think," my roommate tells me. We are watching *Jeopardy!* The contestant is a turtleneck-wearing woman ("A definite loser," my roommate proclaims). I want the woman to win.

She rings the buzzer, pauses before stating the answer in the form of a question. Silence. "What is a tadpole?" I mouth to myself. I feel myself beside her, shifting behind the podium. I want to lean over and say, "It's okay. No one has all the answers."

Alex Trebek's mouth is slightly open and I expect him to say, "I'm sorry, stupid—your time is up." Could he say that on TV? Do they just edit those parts out? Maybe he's right, maybe up to this point it's been luck.

I shrug my shoulders and say, "Give up."

I grab the remote control, turn the channel so I don't have to hear the woman say, "I don't know" or the *you're wrong* buzzer that blocks out voices and music and breathing.

"It's okay," I say. "There are some things not worth knowing."

29

CONVERSION CLASSES

YOUR MOTHER CALLS TO SAY YOUR COUSIN'S HUSBAND IS BECOMING
Catholic. You cradle the receiver against your shoulder and
rearrange the condiments in your fridge door. Your cousin had
no idea he was taking conversion classes, she says, can you
imagine that? You toss a sticky mustard container into the
garbage and wonder why your husband keeps putting balsamic
vinegar in the fridge. You assure your mother you are listening
and repeat the words: Sacraments of Initiation at St. Cecilia's,
Easter Sunday. You pull the cap off the dry-erase pen with your
teeth, write SECOND COMING AT ST. CECILIA'S, EASTER on the white
board beside the phone and agree this is a blessing.

Your husband was baptized, but no longer goes to Mass—
except for Christmas, which he likes, and Good Friday, which
he doesn't. The endless kneeling, he laughs. Up and down and
up and down, it's enough to make you pass out. You have

fainted twice, both times on Good Friday during the reading of the Passion. When Father Julian gets to the part where they cut Jesus's side, and then the water and the blood and the sharp cabbage breath of the woman beside you with the lazy eye, the too-high singing voice become too much. A kaleidoscope of light swirls before you, which would be a comfort if you could focus, lift your heavy hands. You awake in the foyer, staring at Sister Stephanie's thin wooden cross swinging towards you until she clutches it to her chest. She strokes your hot face with a thin cool hand. A powerful day, isn't it, dear? Your husband kneels beside you, his hand on his own forehead, unaware he yanked your dress above your waist as he carried you behind the pews and out the chapel door. Your faded blue, polka dot, silk panties are visible, the ones you told him to wash by hand and he forgot, put them in the washer anyway.

You are wearing the same panties the day you find your wedding dress. In a store called *Precious*. The sort of place that promises class, then asks you to remove your shoes and check large purses at the counter. Your mother crouches in the store entrance and pulls off her brown loafers, says, Let's separate and meet in twenty minutes—trust me, I'm an expert. You smile at her over a display of pearl-studded veils and headpieces adorned with silk flowers as she hoists an off-the-shoulder gown triumphantly and mouths: Success. You think, a smarter woman wouldn't have brought her mother wedding dress shopping. That woman is by herself in a vintage dress shop, trusting her own instincts. That woman is slipping into a simple empire-waist gown, smiling at her reflection in the large three-way mirror of her private change room.

You picture this woman as you stand in the communal dressing room lined with padded benches and sheets of mirror, beside a large woman with a shiny face and wispy brown hair whose mother cries each time she tries a dress. She dabs a tissue into the corner of each perfectly lined eye. Honey, suck in your stomach. Stand on your tiptoes. Don't rest your arms on your sides—remember arm fat. Gasp. Tissue, please. Your mother glances at that mother, hands you a princess-waist dress and rolls her eyes. This dress has pearl beading around the neck and your mother says, Honey, it's subtle, just try it. She clutches her hands to her chest. Is that not perfect? It is so perfect. Excuse me for intruding, the crying mother says, I love it too. Is that your daughter? She's so beautiful. A tissue?

You take this as an omen. Your mother never cries and you never wear white. You swore you'd pick a cream dress, one that didn't reach the floor and had no beads. You had friends with dresses so ornate that on their wedding day they were hard to hug. They moved in a blur of teeth and pearls, touching shoulders and whispering, Thank you. You smile at your mother in the mirror—convinced she's hoping you'll look the same way.

— Do we have to go to the baptism?
— Yes.
— Can we—
— Can we what? Can we just call instead? Can *I* just go alone with my mother?
— Calm down.
— We will not be one of *those* couples.
— What couples?
— The ones where the wives show up to everything and say, *Oh, Bob was feeling a bit under the weather.*
— My throat *does* feel a bit sore.
— Come here.
— Ouch.

You are looking through the glovebox for a piece of gum when you tell your husband you want to go to New Orleans for Mardi Gras. He asks, Like that documentary where women flashed their boobs at the Mardi Gras parade for strings of beads? You only lasted five minutes on our honeymoon without a bikini top. —Am I burning? Are my nipples burning? Do you see anyone we know? Doesn't *he* look like our dry cleaner at home, except with hair?

It's your second day in Bora Bora and a woman from New York with breasts as big as watermelons lies topless by the pool. Marketing, she tells the man beside her as she lathers her left breast with suntan lotion. —I make brochures, Web sites, billboard ads, that sort of thing. You peer over the top of your sunglasses and try to picture her in a business suit, each of her breasts straining against the thin rayon of her corporate blouse. Mama, your husband says enthusiastically in your ear. The woman's breasts glow hot and pink by late afternoon and you say, That's what happens when you're exposed for too long. You pretend to read your magazine and watch with envy the French and Italian mothers with babies and bellies and oversized sunglasses as they oil their sturdy, dark breasts. Your husband claims he likes your pale, tender flesh best.

Celeste, the hostess in the main dining room, has lemon-coloured hair, which reaches the middle of her back; she flips pieces over her shoulders as she tells your husband he has lovely blue eyes. You teasingly call her his girlfriend. But before supper you spend an hour getting dressed, tying and retying your sarong according to the colourful diagram on the small square of gift-shop cardboard. The sarongs in the picture make those women look sexy like Celeste, not gift-wrapped like you. You pour yourself another glass of white wine and adjust the material in front of the mirror. Your husband slips off the bed and rubs your shoulders. When you lived in your own apartment, you dressed alone, tossing belts and scarves in a frustrated heap. There was no one to comment. Your cheeks flush and you want to push him away. Instead, you ask him to hang up the thick terry cloth bathrobe that sits at your feet, the one he presented to you unceremoniously on your wedding night. You bought him a wallet. You both agree practical presents are best, so why can't you stop thinking about the silver hoop earrings you really wanted the birthday he bought you an AMA membership, saying, I'll renew it every year, okay?

You clean out your spare bedroom. You usually keep this door closed and when you open it, a pleasing burst of cool air blasts your face. You kneel in front of the closet with your clear blue recycling bag and yank on pant legs and skirt hems until you have formed a pile. You pretend you are getting ready for an extended houseguest and, therefore, must be ruthless. You have so much in storage: a second (and third) wok, a clear plastic shower curtain embossed with goldfish (it matched the orange shag carpet in your first apartment), boxes of mugs with pictures of hummingbirds (they match an incomplete set of dishes you left in your parents' basement). You have already given much away. But one more box will make you feel freer. You have a friend whose downtown apartment contains only a denim-covered loveseat, a metal bar stool, a blue air mattress and a silver gooseneck lamp. Total freedom, she says. She has a better job than you, but seldom buys anything. You shop with her once when she's replacing her black dress pants. All I need is one pair, she says, walking out of the change room. How else could I afford so many Mexico trips? Now as you look for something, anything, to stuff into the blue bag and mark with an X for the Community Living Foundation that calls for monthly donations of gently used clothes and small household items, you admire her vigilance and try to banish sentimentality. You remind yourself that last month you gave away a black jacket you liked, and then spent an hour the following Saturday digging through racks of pink trench coats and maternity capes at Value Village, hoping to find that jacket on the $10-or-less rack. This time you promise your husband you won't get desperate to donate; you'll choose more carefully. You throw in clothes of his you've always hated. The brown sweatshirt that makes him look round, and the faded blue jeans that are too high in the waist. How can he miss them if he doesn't even know they're gone?

You find your wedding dress in the closet. Not *find,* really, you knew it was there all along. You discover it the way people discover the courage to clip fingernails on new babies or say the word *forever.* Feel the fear and do it anyway, you read somewhere, and wonder why things that are easy to say are never easy to do. You slip out of your jeans and take your wedding dress off its pink quilted hanger. Pull it over your black socks and blue cotton panties, twist your arm behind your back and hold your breath as you pull the tiny zipper. It moves smoother than you expect, and you are surprised at how good you look. That it fits. You sigh laboriously. Everything about you is so different now, from the colour of your hair (French Roast Brown) to the way you give certain advice (ask for a refund—it shouldn't be unravelling). How could your body be exactly the same? You remember that you forgot to have the dress dry-cleaned immediately following the wedding, like you were supposed to. It was hot that day and the church had no air conditioning. The lilies drooped and you sweated, but the armpits of the dress are not yellowed, as you might have expected. You press the smooth fabric to your nose and are comforted that one year later the delicate scent of Escape lingers. When the car lights flood the bedroom window, you take the dress off quickly. You don't want to hear your husband say he still loves the way the dress exposes your collarbones and those small nodules at the base of your neck where your hair rests. You'd rather hear him say that the dress doesn't suit you anymore— that it's too confining. You want to hear him say that you'd be a different bride now. Just a simple cream sheath dress, loose hair, open-toed sandals.

— Would you have converted for me?

— I *am* Catholic.

— A lapsed Catholic—you aren't even confirmed.

— *You*, Ms. Catholic, didn't even want to go to the marriage prep classes.

— That's different.

— How?

— I just thought they'd be different. I just thought it would all be different.

Waiting for your first marriage preparation course, you sit holding your future husband's hand on the host couple's dark brown couch, its armrest doilies crisply starched with scalloped edges. Trays of mini sausage rolls, Nanaimo bars and butter cookies cover the small coffee table. You rub your foot over the criss-cross pattern left by the vacuum and watch the host wife pour tea from a white ceramic pot into delicate teacups— different months of the year written in script on each saucer. The host husband keeps readjusting himself in his chair. You smile politely and compliment their immaculate home. Three words for you, honey, the host wife says—hire a maid. You laugh nervously as she carefully hands you a teacup. Your saucer says October (your mother's birthday) and your future husband's says May (yours), and you'd ask him to trade if you didn't think it would seem petty. I got spring, your future husband says, and you got Hallowe'en—spooky. The host wife starts the evening with the Lord's Prayer, and you motion to your future husband to cross himself. She informs you both, smiling, that she and the host husband were separated for six months two years ago, and they feel the experience better prepared them to counsel couples awaiting marriage. You think *awaiting* is a strange word to use, as though you are not frenzied, talking with the caterer, who says she won't serve just fish, or attending a third dress fitting where the seamstress assures you that you *will* be able to breathe once the bodice seams are loosened.

By week four you are discussing *The Power of Expectation and Assumption.* You read, *The questions on the back of this page are meant to identify our assumptions. But remember, as we are free to keep our present expectations, we are also free to make changes to our ways of thinking to ensure a happier partnership.* You and your future husband sit alone at the host couple's kitchen table, eating mini bagel pizzas, drinking raspberry tea and completing your worksheets. *This tendency to presume that others see things our way is called projection,* he reads aloud. You smile at him, take another sip of raspberry tea.

(1) I think I should be able to spend_____dollars without consulting my spouse after we marry. You write $300 confidently, but then claim the *three* is in fact a messy *one* when your future husband says $50. *(2) When do I think our first child will be born?* You skip this question. *(3) My assumption about weekend worship is that we will_____.* And this one too. Later in the car, you tell your future husband that you can discuss these questions when you've both had more time to think.

You have supper at your favourite Vietnamese restaurant one month before your wedding. As your future husband hangs both your jackets on the wooden coat rack, you see the host wife in a booth with a man. You recognize the back of her head, her tight coppery curls. You catch her reflection in the mirrors that line the restaurant walls and see her face. The way her body curves toward this man. The way she touches her neck every time she speaks. You sit across the restaurant. Your eyes meet momentarily and you look away. You dip your salad roll into fish sauce and tell yourself she'll come over and introduce the man as her co-worker. She doesn't.

You decide to send your cousin's husband an on-line card, but can't find one appropriate for the occasion. Happy Conversion? Happy Transformation? Happy Metamorphosis? Happy Rebirth? Happy Sanctification? Congratulations on your upcoming baptism and confirmation?

You are sitting on the futon in the basement—your bed until you could afford a real one—not watching the TV flickering in the corner and explaining to your husband why you want to drive to Vancouver alone to visit an old friend. Couples do this all the time, you say, take separate vacations. He shakes his head and says, How can you drive to Vancouver alone when you have trouble unlocking the gas cap on the car? I worked with a woman who drove her Jeep Wagoneer to Whitehorse alone and *her* boyfriend called her adventurous and brave, you say. Someone driving to Vancouver with an AMA membership and a cell phone is neither. Someone like *that* can drive anywhere she wants. You can still smell the butter on the popcorn kernels as you collect the bowls and bottles from the table and walk upstairs. Your husband shouts, Why are you referring to yourself in the third person? This is the same way you told him you were quitting your job. If, for instance, *someone* is unfulfilled in her career and has a clear sense of what she wants to do, she should do it—of course, taking her spouse into consideration.

You load the dishwasher—rearrange bowls, rinse chunks of lettuce off dinner dishes he loaded earlier, and remove the Tefal pots that he's already ruined. He makes you a cup of green jasmine tea and sets up the Scrabble board on the kitchen island. You dry your hands on a tea towel and quickly spell OX off the end of his PHOENIX. He claims you are too impetuous, not committed enough, and it's why you seldom win. You remember your mother on Sundays in the kitchen as you played Trivial Pursuit with your father in the next room. You tugged on her pants and said, Please, please come sit down, but settled for putting a brown teddy bear in her place. She never sat down, and now you imagine she's probably like you and prefers the warm, lemon-scented privacy of doing dishes.

— I'm becoming my mother.
    — Does that mean I'm becoming your father or my father?
    — Seriously, I'm answering these marriage prep questions like my mother would.
    — Like what?
    — *What component is most essential to a good marriage: friendship, intimacy, trust, or passion?*
    — Intimacy. No, passion.
    — Friendship—I said friendship, my mother would say friendship.
    — You *are* my very best friend.
    — Shut up.
    — See—passion.

You are on your way out the door when your mother calls. You stand on the doormat, sorting through bills, and answer *no* to all her questions. Do you know what you are wearing to the baptism? Do you want to go shopping, then? Do you want to borrow my mauve dress? You know, the silk one with the pearl buttons. Are you just being difficult? You'll want to look your best, she says, I'll drop off my mauve dress.

Before you meet a friend for coffee, you spend fifteen minutes putting your hair in pigtails, the kind that sit low on your head and make you look trendy and young. You wear the silver hibiscus-shaped earrings your mother gave you as a teenager, the ones that used to jingle whenever you moved your head. You snipped the extra dangling pieces off with wire cutters. Your husband called you crazy for ruining perfectly good earrings, but sat beside you on the bathroom counter and rasped the exposed edges smooth. You meet your friend in a tiny café with old velvet couches, thin woollen rugs, and the smell of cedar incense and burnt coffee. You choose a deep red chair and sink below the armrests, hoping the guy on the bar stool with the sideburns and the thumb ring is smiling at you and not your pigtails. Your girlfriend plunks herself down and says, You look precious with those piggy tails, as she fiddles with your left earring. You smile and ask yourself why you don't call her more often. You're on your second sip of coffee when she says, I'm living with a bush pilot, we met six weeks ago. He's perfect, he plays in a jazz band, has two Dobermans and cut my first initial into his chest with an exacto knife the night we met. Three cups of coffee later, she adds nonchalantly that her boyfriend looks exactly like your husband. You walk down the street outside the café and she is holding your hand as you try to picture your husband as a bush pilot instead of a civil engineer, as someone dangerous. You ask her, Is it like they could be brothers, or only distant cousins? Even in your platform sandals you are slightly shorter. She grabs your shoulders, kisses your forehead enthusiastically and says, You are so funny, married lady—I just love you. Out of sight, you stop and look at yourself in the window of a used bookstore, pull the ponytails out of your hair and shake your head violently from side to side. By the time you reach your car, your hands are shaking from the coffee and you remind yourself that even one cup makes you edgy.

— Do I seem different?

— Different how?

— Do I still seem fun and adventurous—like someone you'd call about a rave or where to buy pot?

— But you don't smoke pot.

— Just answer the question.

— No, you don't seem like that.

— No, I *don't* seem fun and adventurous?

— No, the pot thing—God, you've never even smoked a cigarette.

— I could have.

After two bottles of red wine, your husband tells his friend about an expensive dress you only wore once. Too low cut, he laughs, drawing a modest scoop across your throat with his finger. You laugh too. Try it on, his friend says playfully. You bought the chocolate-coloured wraparound dress for your cousin's baby's christening, and when you picked up your mother she said, Ooh sexy. You figured she was being funny, but the sound of the word filled the car and for the rest of the day you pretended to play with your pearl necklace. At the christening, your mother admired the pink baby and your cousin's simple black pantsuit, the way it minimized her swollen chest. Something like *that* would be obscene if you were a lactating mother, she said, eyeing your cleavage. You sold the dress that winter in a consignment store, which your husband wouldn't understand, so you take your glass of red wine upstairs and come down in your iridescent green high school graduation dress instead. Strapless, a neckline so low you had to dig your black bustier out of the bottom drawer of your dresser, the drawer that contains the champagne-coloured negligee you forgot to pack for your honeymoon and the silky thong underwear you purchased before realizing you aren't a thong underwear person. The underwire on the bustier digs into your armpits. Your husband's eyes widen as he gulps his wine, but his friend smiles approvingly.

For months after, your husband asks you to put the green dress on before you have sex. It's like we're dating again, he says. You don't like the way it reminds you of a girl you worked with whose boyfriend convinced her to shave off her pubic hair to spice things up. He said, You feel like someone new. Sometimes you catch her scratching in the ladies room, her hand down the front of her skirt. She says she'll think twice about doing it again. Again? Your husband says, Weird, and wonders if you'd ever do the same. You decide he's being rhetorical, kiss the top of his head and add more milk to your tea.

You try to look unfettered when the woman tells you about the shaving—sitting in the passenger seat of her new Volkswagen—the way you do when she recounts the night she is drunk and kisses Jill in accounting. She says women's lips are more delicate than men's. She smiles, calls you beautiful, and you are afraid she might kiss you too. You keep this secret from your husband, along with the fact that you forgot to wear your wedding band the weekend you took CPR certification, that you kissed your brother-in-law on the lips by mistake on New Year's Eve.

You are lying on your bed, looking at the ceiling as you dial your cousin's number. I heard about the new convert, you say enthusiastically into the phone. He's going to be baptized too, hey? At least he's big enough; you won't need to hold his head over the baptismal font. You fold up the map of Vancouver you had spread across the bed and swing your feet over the side. Tell him that if he changes his mind, fainting doesn't work; the priest will take it as a sign of overwhelming faith. If he's a good little soldier we'll bring him chocolate Easter eggs instead of a rosary. You hang up, stuff the map in your bottom drawer and wonder if women with babies and newly baptized husbands collect street maps of places they'd like to go.

You are admiring your now sparse storage closet. You climb inside, sit cross-legged on a square of blue carpet and look up at black garment bags and thin plastic covers that contain clothes you are not ready to give away. But from where you are sitting, the closet looks crowded and you wonder if you should reconsider keeping your cream and red sundress, your navy blue skirt and your black linen pants, their hems resting on your shoulders.

You lie in bed until noon on Saturday and decide that if you don't get up you won't feel pressured to go with your mother to the funeral of her neighbour's aunt. She calls Friday, saying, Your father isn't feeling up to it and, besides, us woman are better at small talk. In your mind you scream, It's not admirable to only be good at surface conversation. But you say, Maybe, and write TOTAL STRANGER'S FUNERAL below NAIL POLISH REMOVER on your whiteboard.

Downstairs, you hear the clink and sizzle of your husband making coffee and eggs. Your weekend routine—he ate hours ago as he read *The Globe and Mail* and will soon come up with breakfast and tell you about the stories he's read. He fixates on the sad ones involving children being mistreated or even killed, and recounts the events in subdued tones, his forehead wrinkled, eyes clear and deliberate. You listen to him as you eat your eggs and ask questions like, where was the baby boy's father? (at work), how cold was it? (-17) and how did they get him off the balcony? (they didn't). He moves the empty serving tray, tosses the paper beside the bed and slips into the crumb-filled sheets for a quick nap. You have never known another adult who gets tired when he is sad. He is ten when his grandfather dies, his sobbing mother hangs up the phone, piles her four children on top of the plaid comforter of her queen-sized bed in the middle of a hot summer afternoon, and hums "Moon River" until they drift off. He says he always feels better when he wakes up—even if he only sleeps for a few minutes. You yelled at him to stop asking if you wanted to take a nap the morning you packed for your grandmother's funeral, but now you lie beside him, hold his hand and watch him sleep. A web of blue veins barely perceptible through his pale skin as his chest rises and falls.

— You want me to get confirmed, then?

— No—that's not it.

— Then what's the big deal?

— I just feel that getting married has changed me more than you.

— *I've* gained more weight.

— Is that supposed to make me feel better?

— You could start smoking pot—would that make you feel better?

— Why won't you take me seriously?

It's Sunday. Conversion day. You are wearing your mother's mauve silk A-line. You study yourself in the full-length mirror and think the A-line makes you look like somebody else; somebody more contented, more accepting, more compliant. You push your hands down the sides of the skirt. Decide the thin fabric will smooth with control-top pantyhose. You walk towards the full-length mirror, you walk away. Rip off the silky folds and grab the green dress with the flared skirt your husband thinks looks like peppermint antacid. You pull it on, stand on your tiptoes. You pirouette. You twirl. Forget the pantyhose. You're ready. You grab the duffel bag you packed last night and head downstairs. One hour and your cousin's husband will take the wafer on his tongue and transform himself into a brand new person. One hour and you'll be driving west, listening to Alanis Morissette and maybe even smoking a cigarette.

BELONGINGS

_____

MY MOTHER'S HAIR IS THE FIRST THING I STEAL FROM THE BASEMENT.
She is examining bulk foods for expiration dates and tossing
them into blue recycling buckets—one bound for the garbage,
the other for the food bank.

"Christ, Mum, what's this?" I wave the bag out in front of
me with two fingers. My mother straightens from her crouched
posture on the floor, a position she says will protect her back
when lifting things. "Pull it out."

"What the hell is it?"

"Just pull it out." She laughs, turning to pitch a large bag of
rotini pasta into the food bank bucket.

"It looks like a dead animal."

"It's human, I assure you."

"Jesus—"

She grabs the bag from me and empties it out on the carpet.

"See, human. Hair. My hair." The two shiny black plaits fall out of a plastic bag along with hard plastic rosary beads and a yellowed communion photograph, in which the tight braids hang neatly down her ten-year-old back. She thrusts the plaits towards me. I grab one, cautiously. It is tied together at the top and bottom with brown shoelaces. It starts out thick, then tapers down to a thin glossy curl that extends an inch past the second shoelace. With one hand I hold the pieces of wiry hair that sprout out the top and slip the other hand down its bumpy ridges, surprised at how alive it feels. My mother snatches the plait from me, holds both of them at the base of her cropped hair—the only length I remember her having.

"Can you believe it," she says, examining the hair closely, "that this beautiful hair belonged to me?" She scratches her fingers across the top of her head, through the small patches of exposed scalp where her hair springs apart. Those spots she calls *holes* that she makes me check for before we get out of the car on our weekly shopping trips to the mall. She passes me the braids and turns around for me to cover the *holes*. I move my fingers slowly through her coarse hair, pulling curls back into place, hiding as much grey as possible, wrapping individual curls around my index finger, smoothing them with my thumb.

"I better get a decent cut and colour before I move," my mother says. It was her idea to move back to the Bahamas. After my father retired and my grandmother fell and broke her leg for the second time, my mother informed me, "It's time to go home."

She sighs deeply, letting me know she wants me to stop fussing with her hair, that she needs to get back to work. I continue to stroke her head with my fingertips. Over the years my mother and I have worked out a silent arrangement: she will only indulge my need for physical affection when it comes to matters of life and death, or air travel.

"Maybe you should shave your head," I say, turning away from her with the plaits. "You could grow new hair for your new start."

"Do you want this pasta sauce? It's good for another few months."

"No," I say, rubbing a braid against my cheek. "Can I keep them?" I clutch them to my chest.

"No, I'm going to keep those for posterity," she says, as if *posterity* were a person, an old friend she might like to show silly things from the past. "Just put them in one of those boxes." She motions to the small stack in the corner labelled for shipping. She turns away to finish her food sorting and I tuck the hair into the corner of my box, the one that holds the blackened teakettle and the straw placemats I rescued from the basement sale pile. *Posterity*, I mouth sarcastically behind my mother's back.

The basement sale is two days away. My mother is expecting anywhere from five to twenty people. All friends of Vivy's, the woman who runs the herbal store my mother frequents. Families just arrived from Korea and a number of Korean immigrants who have been here a couple of years, many of whom were taken in by family or friends and could not afford to bring many possessions with them.

"We have lots of furniture to sell—practically new," she says, winking at me from her spot on the kitchen floor. She squeezes the phone between her head and shoulder, craning her neck as she cuts handles into the side of another cardboard box. "They must have forgotten to punch handles in the whole bunch," she whispers to me under her breath. "No, sorry, I'm talking to my daughter. No, no, she doesn't live here. Yes, she's married. She's helping me pack." She laughs and winks again.

I sit down and motion to her to pass the utility knife and the box. She disregards me, waves the knife through the air as she speaks. "There is also a leather couch and loveseat. Black. And then knick-knacks and some clothing. Yes, good prices. Okay, super, see you Thursday, 7:00 p.m. Yes, you too. Okay, bye-bye." She hangs up the phone and resumes cutting.

"Be careful," I say as she makes a deep slice in the cardboard while looking around for the next thing to be done.

"That was Vivy. Ouch." She licks a small drop of blood off her finger. "You know, the Korean one?" Lately, my mother has increased the frequency with which she asks rhetorical questions. *That hammer might be handy—don't you think? You don't mind coming over to go through a few more things—do you? You don't mind coming to spend Christmas in Nassau this year?*

"What are you going to sell?" I look at the boxes with my name on them, the ones my mother told me I will now have to store at my apartment.

"There's only so much your father and I can fit in that shipping container. And besides, we'll be living with family to begin with, so we won't need much right away." She rubs her hands down her thighs, rocking back and forth on the balls of her feet.

"Sim-plif-ication," she says as if she has just discovered how to speak another language. "Okay, we need to get to work on this sorting and pricing." She claps her hands and hops up from the floor, faster than I imagine my half-asleep legs could move. "Where can we get those price stickers? Staples? Wal-Mart, I suppose." She's into another cupboard, digging through dull pots and pans. "Look at this," she shouts triumphantly, "a perfectly good wok. I forgot we had this. They'll love this. We'll wash it up and presto. Do you think we'll need a float? Like a bank float, small bills and that. Or do you think they'll use cheques? Maddie, are you listening?"

"Yes, Mother," I dig through a box labelled *Madeleine's School Work*, sorting through piles of coloured drawings and elementary school workbooks.

"Your father pulled those out from under the stairs," she says. Most of the books are from the second grade, my first year at West Dalhousie Elementary. One book is filled with journal entries. I read the titles aloud, "My First Day in Calgary, Alberta, Canada, The Day I Went to Lake Louise and the

Mountains, A Drive to Fun Fort Whoop-up, Our Long Christmas Visit to the Bahamas, The First Day I Saw Snow."

It is obvious from the stories that my mother and father must have helped me write them, the curve of my lettering too precise, as if traced from someone else's practised script. And the language, the words *incredible* and *majestic* make me sound more competent than I remember being that first year, when I couldn't get it straight whether to go home at recess or lunchtime. I'd hear a bell and be off running across the schoolyard and up the hill, eventually realizing that no one was behind me, no one passing me on that curve just before the pedestrian crossing where I'd usually tire and slow to a walk. "Not again," my mother would say through the screen door, "it's not lunchtime yet." She would walk me back to school, where I would sit red and teary-eyed on the small corner of the piano bench next to big Mrs. Dill, my music teacher, who would squeeze my leg affectionately and say, "You're just brand new."

"You should keep those schoolbooks," my mother says, now up on a stepladder, looking in the cupboard above the fridge.

"Will's mother kept all of his childhood stuff," I say, pushing the box against the wall, "she has an entire room dedicated to mementoes—she made labels on the computer for every box."

"That's impressive." My mother clatters plates and serving dishes on top of the fridge. "An organized woman. Now, do you think those people will buy this?" She doesn't bother to turn around, holds out an old Formica cutting board with a conch shell on it, balancing herself against the fridge. She brought the board from the Bahamas. It was the only one she used for years after we moved to Calgary, long after she and my father could have afforded a new one. I used to think it was homesickness, that using the same cutting board was one less thing that had changed. But when she replaced it with another Formica board, one with a moose and the words *Banff, Canada* in fancy script, I knew it was only surface and not meaning that mattered. I stare at the conch board and then the back of my mother's hair, surprisingly unkempt—a ring of white against her black curls.

"Careful, Mother, your roots are showing."

She steps down from the ladder and tosses the cutting board into the garbage.

"Another box?" my husband says, barely looking up from his magazine at the kitchen table. It is late and the kitchen light, which I have wanted to replace since we moved in, casts a dull hue over the apartment.

"There's not *too* much," I say and kick the apartment door with my foot and slip the box out of the hallway. This is the eighth box I have brought from my mother's house. The crawl space above the closet in our second bedroom is the only storage we have and in one week I have filled it with books, photographs, clothes and blankets, and I have also imposed a collection of porcelain eggs and crystal dishes on the usually sparse décor of our apartment.

"Is this stuff emotional or practical?" He raises his eyebrows and leans back in his chair, trying to peek around the closet door.

"Pardon me?" I say, ignoring the labels he applies to each item I have brought from my parents' house. "It's really not that much. Just some kitchen stuff and . . . a wooden man I want to put in our bedroom," I say quickly, hoping he will go back to his magazine.

"A wooden man." He shakes his head. "How big are we talking?" He holds his hands about one foot apart, slowly moving them further and further away from one another.

"It's nice." I look through the box. "I mean, it's not . . . I thought we could put it on the floor in our bedroom."

"A giant wooden man in our bedroom?"

My husband is not terribly inspired in his decorating style, accepting most changes I make to our home with a placid *Is this new?* or an uninterested *Was that always there?* When we moved in together there was nothing in his seven packing boxes he insisted had to be displayed in the apartment. In the last several days, for the first time, he has developed concerns: *This tortoiseshell is not staying here. Your mother could sell this plant stand at that weird basement sale of hers. We already have ugly brown dishes.*

"Let's see this man then," he says and holds a hand out in front of him.

"I couldn't really carry it with the box." I look at the floor. "Can you hold the downstairs door for me?"

"Jesus." He slips on his shoes, stuffs a fleece hat and mitts under his arm and walks out the door and down the stairs, saying, "This should be good."

We walk across the parking lot, the snow crunching under our boots. I unlock the rear door of the car and bend in to where I have securely wedged the man between the driver's seat and the back seat. It is made of madeira wood—a plain face with a broad nose and a gentle smile. There is a deep crack in the back of the head, threatening to split it in two. "Careful." I cradle it in my arms. "It's a little damaged."

Will looks at it. "This is hideous." Then at me. "Please tell me you're joking."

I slam the car door and pull the wooden man out of his arms. Despite its weight, I move quickly towards the door, holding it close to my chest.

"In all the years I have known your family, I have never seen that thing," he shouts ahead to me. "You probably never knew they had it. Don't you have to have known that something existed for it to have sentimental value?" His words in the crisp, dry air sound louder than I imagine he intended.

I stumble on the landing, instinctively cupping the wooden man's head with my hand.

"Look, there's either a conch shell or a sand dollar in every room of our apartment. And those decorative plates above the kitchen cupboards," he pauses, softening when he catches up to me and sees my weary face, "you hate decorative plates."

Inside, we sit on the apartment building stairs. "Put it in the bedroom if it means that much to you," he says and strokes my shoulders. I lay the wooden man beside us and stare into his unfamiliar face. An inscription has been written into the bottom. My mother has blacked most of it out with marker, probably in the hopes of selling it at her basement sale. I cannot make out the words; there is an *H* or a *P* or an *R*.

Upstairs, I call my mother, who cannot remember what the inscription said. "I don't know," she says firmly as if shutting a cupboard door left absentmindedly open. "It was some kind of going-away present from a neighbour in Nassau. We never took it out of storage when we arrived here. I never really liked it—it's just too much."

I feel my face flushing. "You scratched the inscription out without reading what it said?" I hang up, lay the wooden man on the kitchen table and apply lemon oil with a soft cloth, hoping to stop the crack from spreading further.

By the middle of the week white sheets of paper are delicately taped to the walls of my parents' house, each designating an area and destination for the items that sit below. The signs are written in all-caps, a hurried script that has more flair than my mother's usually careful hand. There is the kitchen with two designated areas, KITCHEN (TO BAHAMAS) and KITCHEN (FOR KOREANS). There is the master bedroom, which has small white stickers with the abbreviation KOR. stuck on the headboard of the oak bed frame and the other pieces of bedroom furniture. The hallway is lined with stacks of *National Geographic* and *Fine Homebuilding*, the lopsided sign reading MAGAZINES (TO USED BOOKSTORE), a small KOR. scrawled in the bottom corner with a question mark.

"I have a system," my mother says as she drags a lawn chair

down the basement stairs. "S . . . P . . . A . . . C . . . E. Space—it's an acronym."

"For what?" I ask, tossing my mittens and coat in the front foyer, as far away from COATS (FOR CHARITY) as possible.

"Sort," she shouts from the bottom of the stairs. "Purge. Assign. Containerize. And—"

"Evacuate?" I reply.

"What's that?"

"Never mind." I walk downstairs and study the mishmash of items spread out on the floor. "So what does the E stand for?"

"Evaluate or Enumerate, or something."

My mother stands, hands on hips, assessing the basement like a general in a battlefield. "I've sent your father to the dump with all that old wood and drywall he had stashed away in the garage. That should keep him busy. He's slowing me down, and we need to get going."

"When do the new people move in?"

"Two weeks." My mother opens the storage space under the stairs that holds dozens of suitcases. "Now, we've got to fill these up for the charities."

I stare at her, trying to imagine my parents, Will and me squeezed around the table of our small apartment two weeks from now, eating supper, sharing a bathroom until moving day—wishing they'd left a week early. Wishing they'd never leave. I exhale and join her in front of the storage space. Each suitcase is covered in stickers, the colourful sort we used to get each time we travelled to the Bahamas for summer holidays or Christmastime. The edges curl and the adhesive balls up in gooey pieces where the stickers have shifted over time.

"Are you going to take these suitcases?" I ask, fingering the stickers.

"No, just the Samsonites. I'm just going to fill those with charity clothes. This pile is immigrant aid," she says, pointing to the CHARITY #1 sign on the far wall, "and this one's for the handicapped." She points to CHARITY #2.

"Disabled." I unzip a suitcase and place the clothing inside. "God, Mum, some of this stuff—I mean, this is how old?"

"It is all in perfectly good condition," she says, picking up a pair of checked pants with substantial cuffs from the CHARITY #1 collection.

"Those poor kids, in these ridiculous pants."

"Those pants were good enough for you." She lays them along the bottom of the suitcase.

"Clothes like this are the reason you get teased."

"You did not get teased." She holds up a grey pinafore dress. "This was your favourite. Remember?"

I snort and shake my head.

"You were hypersensitive. I made this dress out of a maternity jumper of mine. Did you know that?" She turns it inside out to check the stitching on the hem. "This held up well. Really, you were a good student, you always had lots of friends."

"Here." I grab the dress, tossing it halfway up the stairs. "I want it."

"For what?"

"For Godsakes, Mum, you made the dress. Is it so strange that I might like to keep it?"

She rolls her eyes. "Some refugee child could have gotten good use out of that."

I ignore her and throw a blue and white party dress, the one I wore at my tenth birthday party with an artificial fur stole, beside the grey one. "You know, when we moved here, I'd stay awake at night wondering what would happen if you and Dad died. Who would I call?"

"Leave the rest." She tugs a T-shirt with a cat decal out of my hands. "9-1-1, we had that little sign on the phone, remember?"

"Stop it." I take the shirt back, tuck it under my right leg. "I used to dial Abuela's number just to make sure I knew how to dial long distance by myself."

"She never told me you called." She quickens the pace, shoving the clothes in the suitcase, pausing every now and then to check that the suitcase still closes comfortably.

"I didn't. I mean, I hung up before she answered." I carry a small bundle of clothes over to the stairs, where I fold and stuff them between the railing and the wall. "I just wanted to know that I could call just in case."

"You make it sound like we live in the middle of nowhere." She snaps the suitcase shut and pushes it against the wall. "There. One down." She leans forward to pull a large, brown vinyl bag across the carpet. "Not fifty feet away were neighbours. Very nice people."

"Yes," I smile sarcastically. "Very nice people." I look at her. "Were you scared when we moved?"

"I made you this coat before we arrived here." She smoothes her hand over the brown lining of a small trench coat with brass buttons. "But it was colder than I thought and you never wore it that first winter. After that it was too small. What a waste. You should keep it." She folds it and places it beside me.

I peek out the front curtain and watch the cars round the corner. The snow crackles under the tires as they slow in front of the house. I close the curtain momentarily, watch them through the gauzy white material. Two of the cars park across the street, but the nicest car, the Lexus, parks in the driveway. This must be the herbal lady. Her car is packed with several women and one small child, whom they pass between them as they unload, grabbing handbags, scarves and gloves. I pull the curtain slightly and see an excited cloud of frozen breath rise above their heads as they gather on the driveway. "Your basement sale women are here," I shout back towards the kitchen.

She asks, "How many cups of coffee?"

One woman pulls out a calculator and measuring tape from her pocket. Another nods at her approvingly. "Believe me, they aren't here for the coffee," I say as the doorbell chimes. "Just come and get the door."

"You get it, please. I'm trying to figure out these measurements," she mutters. "I packed the stupid scoop."

They stand expectantly on the landing. A couple of women spill onto the first few steps, they poke their heads through to get a look. "Come in, hello," my mother says from over my shoulder.

"Yes, please come in," I say, stepping back from the entryway.

My mother passes me the coffee can and introduces me to Vivy, who shakes my hand enthusiastically while turning and saying to my mother, "Pretty girl. So lucky." Vivy introduces each woman in the crammed entrance, squeezing through a sea of elbows and knees as they remove their winter boots.

I want to pinch my mother as she repeats their names back to them in the form of a question, "Ch-ung-Hay?" "Soon-Yu-in?" "Lee-lee?"

"Lilly," I correct her. "I think her name is Lilly, Mum, like Lillian."

"Yes, Lillian," shouts Vivy, who then appears to explain something to the woman in Korean.

The women refuse my mother's offer to hang up their coats, insisting, as Vivy translates, that they don't want to interrupt my mother's evening. My mother gives them an appreciative smile, then looks at me as if to say, *See, this won't be so bad.*

She offers them the still-brewing coffee, which Vivy gratefully accepts, wrapping her hands around the glass mug. "So so cold," she says.

"Welcome to Canada, ladies," my mother says and smiles. "Cold," she says slowly, as if it is the first time she has formed the word. She crosses her arms in front of her chest, grabbing her shoulders in mock shiver.

"Mum, they know," I scold. Then change my mind and add, "Never mind, sorry." I smile politely at the women.

A couple of the women wear thick woollen socks and loose-fitting corduroy pants that pool at their ankles, seeming to belong to someone else, someone taller. Others wear only light stockings on their feet, rubbing their feet back and forth on top of one another as they produce exaggerated shudders and grin at my mother. "Pretty house," a woman in a forest green ski jacket says tentatively.

"Yes, yes, pretty," a few others agree. The rest just smile, chat quietly and follow my mother and Vivy through the hallway and down the back stairs, glancing from room to room at carefully stacked boxes and the dismantled furniture with foam affixed to sharp corners and legs. "No, no, upstairs is the stuff we're taking," I hear my mother say with authority. "Not for sale."

We descend the stairs as a group. "Nice. Pretty things," I hear one woman whisper up ahead. My childhood possessions are tagged for five to fifty dollars on the basement floor. There is the jungle-print couch, the black wooden elephant, the peach and green ruffled cushions with matching valances, the hand-knit blue mohair sweaters, the tortoiseshell buffed to a lacquered shine, the brass coffee table with its chipped glass top, the set of red and gold New Caxton encyclopedias, missing letters M to P, all sprawled out on the sea-green carpet, in-between brown cardboard packing boxes, rolls of bubble wrap and worn metal shipping trunks, like spilled freight waiting to be rescued.

In all the years I lived in this house, my mother never had a real garage sale, scoffing at the neighbours as they dragged old tables, lamps and cutlery out on to their driveways at 8:00 a.m. Saturday, waving to her excitedly as she gathered the paper from the front step, *First pick. Neighbour's discount.*

"No shame, I tell you," she'd tell my father over morning tea, "people poking through your personal belongings. Not me, I tell you. Downright embarrassing."

I'm the cashier. I have a metal cash box my mother borrowed from a woman at work, filled with small bills and handfuls of loose coins. I set it on an empty shipping trunk and watch the women mill about, politely lifting vases, figurines, dishes—holding them away from their bodies as if to gain some objectivity. I open and close the money box, double-checking the float, wishing I had a magazine or book, a barrier between me and the basement sale.

"Yes, real tortoiseshell, very expensive," my mother says to a woman wearing bright pink lipstick, to whom Vivy quickly translates. My mother speaks to the woman directly, following Vivy's speech pattern, unconsciously dropping the same words, as if she is trying to make her feel more comfortable.

There is some commotion over by the stationary bike as one woman tries to stretch her feet to reach the pedals. "Too high," Vivy says, giggling.

"Yes, too high," my mother repeats. She attempts to adjust the seat. "Maddie, come here." She motions to me and says, "It's tricky, my daughter knows how." I unscrew the bolt and slip it into the hole closest to the bottom. The woman hops back on and spins her socked feet around at a dizzying pace. The other women laugh and nod approvingly.

"Thirty dollar?" Vivy fingers the white price tag.

"Yes," my mother says quickly, "barely used." She smiles, pats her full behind and laughs knowingly.

"Okay, what about twenty dollar?" Vivy asks, after a brief exchange with the woman on the bike. She hops off the bike and pulls a crisp twenty from her small black pocketbook.

And so it begins. The rowing machine, chesterfield and matching chair, and pine bookcase sell quickly. Some women start claiming sections of wall where they pile up their chosen items, leaving behind a handbag or jacket to stake their claim.

Two women laugh as they try on handmade sweaters, knit by my grandmother, marking each birthday until my sixteenth. I have piled the ones I liked in the back of my already full bedroom closet. The women buy the rest.

I go upstairs to refill Vivy's coffee cup at my mother's request, and find myself rushing back so as not to miss the departure of one single item. I watch them as I sit quietly on the trunk, handing back change, affixing the price stickers of the purchased items to the top of the money box and thinking, *What could you possibly want with the Loony Tunes lamp from my old bedroom? Do you know I once had sex in that sleeping bag? How do you know those curtains will fit your window? Do you know that cassette player makes music sound like it's under water?*

"I feel like a weight is being lifted off me," my mother says giddily, as she grabs Vivy's coffee from me. "All this junk gone and they are actually paying me for it." She smiles and taps the side of the metal box.

"Now, that still works perfectly," she shouts to a woman lightly fingering the silent keys of the Yamaha organ that sits in a corner surrounded by neat stacks of LPs and cassette tapes. "In fact, my daughter can play it for you."

"No," I shout, surprising myself with the force of my refusal. The woman at the organ looks at me, patting the seat gently. "I mean, I haven't played for years. Really, I was never very good."

"She's being modest. She plays wonderfully," my mother says with a kind of pride she only expresses in front of house guests. She grabs the cash box and nudges me towards the organ. I open the bench and dig through music books, looking for something I remember how to play.

Halfway through "Eight Days a Week" I begin to panic. I mess up the end of the chorus and soon I am having trouble reading the music. The notes shift. "That's all I can remember." I spin around on the bench and look at the floor—the cheap Monet reproductions, the frame that once held a picture of my grandmother, the assortment of partly used fabrics and tangled bobbins of thread.

I excuse myself and go upstairs to the bathroom, where I sit on the closed toilet. The din from the basement grows louder and louder, my mother's voice above the rest, "Good good price," and "good good quality." I am washing my face with cold water when I hear them on the stairs and wonder if they could be leaving so soon. Voices growing more and more excited in the hallway outside the door. Against her initial decision, my mother has moved the sale upstairs. I sit back on the toilet, frozen, imagining them opening sealed boxes, looking in the back of closets and rifling through drawers. Something heavy thumps onto the floor and then there's the tearing of packing tape. I can hear my mother say, "I was going to take these, but you know, I'll probably just buy something new when I get home anyway."

As I walk out of the bathroom, I can feel my throat getting tighter. I want to leave. I want to call Will and tell him to bring the car, back it into the driveway and help me load as much as we can in the back.

"What are you doing?" My strained voice rises out of the background. I approach the group huddled in the living room around a stack of addressed and sealed boxes. Vivy is kneeling beside my mother, using her car keys to tear through the tape.

"We make you open all these boxes," she laughs at my mother, who is running a fingernail through the tape on another box.

"Good, Maddie, there you are. Help me undo some of these boxes. Get the knife for those." My mother excitedly motions towards boxes labelled LIVING ROOM (TO BAHAMAS).

"I thought you were going to keep this stuff." I take a deep breath and rub the back of my tight neck. Many of the women have taken off their coats, tied them around their waists for greater mobility. They hunch over the boxes waiting for my mother to reveal pieces of favourite dinnerware, colourful ceramic coasters and crystal salt and pepper shakers.

"Nice, yes?" my mother says. The women nod and move closer to her. They kneel and sit around her, gasping at a collection of embroidered table linens, a Christmas present from my grandmother.

"I so sad for you," a woman in a sand-coloured sweater

whispers to me, clutching the brass vase that my mother used to keep beside her bed, "we take away all your pretty things. We take good good care of them."

I swallow hard. I can't answer her. I walk down the hall to get the knife for my mother and look back at her standing in the middle of the women, her gestures exaggerated as if she is a schoolteacher reading from a picture book. She passes items around the semicircle in front of her and jokes, "Buy one, get one free," as she stuffs bills into her pockets. Her face looks round and shiny like a helium-filled balloon, so full she is about to float away.

Famished

ALISON'S APARTMENT IS ON THE TOP FLOOR. SHE HAS A CONCRETE balcony with a green plastic chair where she sits on days when the sun melts the snow and it seems, for a moment, to shine on her alone. She usually goes inside and makes herself a big cheese sandwich and sits on the couch—a safe distance from the spotlight. Sometimes she stays on the balcony, though, and watches the pink house across the road that no one has come out of, or gone in to, in the four months she has been living here. It is the kind of house she might not ordinarily notice. The kind with an overgrown garden that even in February, with its skinny branches stripped bare, creates a canopy over the backyard in which she can barely make out the silver corner of a tool shed. Or is it a hibernating car? She sees the house first thing this morning, and every morning, from the sliding doors at the end of her dark tunnel of an apartment where she boils water in a blackened saucepan for instant coffee, getting ready for another day as a communications intern at the Department of Family and Social Services.

Alison has a purple fleece housecoat wrapped around her, which she can't afford but bought full price at La Senza last week when the heat went out for the fourth time this winter. "That should do 'er," said her landlord as he banged a wrench on the heating pipes beside her bed.

"Thanks. Again," she mumbled beneath the scarf wrapped around her head like a bandage. The first time the heat stopped, Alison couldn't reach her landlord for days. At first her phone messages were polite, but the last one consisted of her screaming, "I'm freezing to death," and slamming the phone down, her hands shaking with fear or exhilaration—she couldn't decide which.

That week the temperature sunk to -32 and her breath hung like billows of smoke in her apartment. She slept in her toque and ski jacket, heated her hands over the range top in her kitchenette and eventually ran the shower on hot, letting the steam warm the air. The furniture and orange shag carpet released old smells as the hot air curled out from the bathroom into seldom-cleaned corners. Fried bacon and hotdog, a sharp whiff of cat. Alison finally turned the taps off when a brown residue poured down the walls. "Shit, it's like stigmata," said her neighbour Ralph, who found her frantically wiping the walls when he wandered through the door she opened to disperse the stench. She closed it behind him and sat sobbing on her rug, the wispy clouds of steam making her apartment feel like another planet.

This morning she can't tell if the heat's out or if it's just cold, cold, cold like the weatherman said on last night's news. Alison's half-asleep mind is already thinking about coffee break, when she'll get to drink *real* coffee, not Sanka (consistently the cheapest coffee at Hull's Foods). She and Julie, from Environmental Protection, will trudge down Jasper Avenue to the no-name Chinese restaurant where Julie will smoke and tell her about Roger (the asshole from Environment who pretends to start work every morning at 4:00 a.m., claiming he just stepped out for breakfast when Julie arrives to open the office at 7:45 a.m.). "You just wait, I'll booby trap him." Julie tells this story every week, but Alison knows she'll probably never do anything to Roger. Neither would she. Alison will eat a small order of fried dumplings, drizzled with an extra scoop of thick sweet and sour sauce, and listen to Julie anyway. She'll nod and laugh, watching Julie's hand wave her cigarette about, and wish they didn't have to go back into the cold, that they didn't have to go back to work, ever.

The government was one month late with Alison's first paycheque, forcing her to survive the month of November on the flat of sodium-reduced cream of mushroom soup her mother bought her from Costco—insisting she carry it onto the Greyhound so the cans wouldn't get dented in the luggage compartment. "It makes a decent sauce in a pinch," her mother shouted, waving goodbye. Alison didn't ask her parents for money to buy fresh produce. Proud to do it on her own. But she's secretly convinced the lack of vitamins in November resulted in some minor hair loss (or maybe it was the dishwashing liquid she used when she ran out of shampoo). As she pours milk over her corn flakes, she's thinking about those dumplings. She hopes there's something interesting to do at work, like a speech or a news release, so the time will pass quickly and she won't have to sort newspaper clippings again.

Alison eats her breakfast while looking in her walk-in closet, the only other room in her apartment, except for the bathroom. She picks out a grey wool skirt, blue turtleneck sweater and black control-top tights and stuffs them under her duvet to warm. Though she curses the temperamental heating, she likes getting dressed under her bedcovers. She sits in the middle like a giant tent pole, feels for her tights, which she carefully inspects, making sure the seams are on the inside and the extra spandex panel at the front for her tummy. Sitting in her cocoon, Alison enjoys the Mountain Breeze scent of her sheets. She washes them every week, though she supposes that Julie is right, they aren't dirty enough in seven days to warrant the $1.75 load. "Whatever gets you through," Julie says, "I'm just saying that's like an extra latte a week." Alison loves this moment under the covers, when her day hasn't started and nothing has disappointed her and there are still at least three meals to be eaten.

Alison fishes through her laundry basket for a pair of wool socks to insulate her tattered winter boots. She pushes the tops of the socks into her boots so their bright orange stripes don't poke out, wishing she was the kind of woman who wore wide-brimmed hats or velvet capes, not caring if people stare. She stuffs a juice box and a granola bar in her purse, in case she gets stuck in her meeting with the woman from the Office for Community Services and can't meet Julie for the fried dumplings.

On the bus she sees a man who reminds her of George in Calgary, whom she broke up with when she took this job in Edmonton. She wanted to move overseas, but a government internship seemed like a good opportunity at the time (the only one, in fact) and she imagined it was a stepping stone to some international governmental posting (which she's quickly realized it isn't). George laughed when she said she was taking the job, that Edmonton didn't seem so bad, that it was a good career move. But she accepted his offer for a going-away supper her last night. She gulped three spicy Caesars, ate four crusty dinner rolls before her $18.95 lobster penne in sundried tomato cream sauce arrived. By eleven o'clock, when George dropped her at her old apartment, her stomach was already growling. She sat in her apartment, cluttered with cardboard packing boxes, eating green beans and apricots in light syrup with her hands, straight from the cans. She sent George a thank-you card with a picture of daisies and a proverb (*Gratitude is the heart's memory*) to let him know that the can opener he gave her as a housewarming present had come in very handy. Though she swears she's over him, that she made the right choice, she remembers he was good with tools and wonders if he might be able to fix the heat.

At noon she picks up the daily special from the downstairs café and eats in the boardroom with Mandy, the director's executive assistant. Mandy brings videotapes of *The Young and the Restless*, which they watch, surreptitiously, on the VCR that sits in the corner shielded by the door. There is a small group of women, communications officers, that usually goes for lunch. They pass the boardroom window laughing, carrying colourful to-go mugs and daytimers. Alison considers going with them— she's gone before—ordering garden salad with the dressing on the side. Desperate to get back to work where she can sit on the heating vent next to her office window and eat one (or two) of the peanut butter and marmalade bagels she has stored in a Ziploc bag at the back of her filing cabinet.

Alison likes eating with Mandy, who watches *The Young and the Restless* so intently she wouldn't notice, or care, if Alison ate a half pan of lasagne with her bare hands, and she certainly wouldn't care that Alison's skirt is held together with a safety pin. Sometimes Alison feels guilty eating in the boardroom, she could be in her own office jotting down things-to-do on a legal sized pad of paper, listing goals, planning her days. She promises herself that tomorrow she will spend her lunch hour transcribing her appointments and meetings onto Microsoft Outlook from the frame of yellow sticky notes around her computer monitor. She has been reluctant, up to this point, to catalogue and account for her days, afraid that once displayed in neat rows of Times New Roman, the information will confirm what she has always feared, that she has little of any consequence to do. She used to log onto Outlook to view the packed appointment schedules of other people in the office, checking for a block of time her office neighbour was away and she could call Julie to chat. She thought herself clever for figuring out how to do this, until she realized people could tell she was checking their calendars. They would poke their heads around her door to ask, "Do you have a question?" or "Can I help you with something?"

Months ago, Julie told Alison that she is trying to get pregnant. Julie and her boyfriend Robbie live in a house with two other people while Robbie finishes his art diploma. Julie figures a baby might be the push they need to find a place of their own. She books an appointment each month at her doctor's office that she cancels when she gets her period. Alison goes to these appointments with Julie, times when Julie is several days late, both terrified and excited, and doesn't want to receive the news alone. Alison flips through the waiting room *Flare*, relieved when Julie appears teary-eyed in the waiting room, looking to Alison for comfort. The two of them linking arms as they ride the glass elevator down to the street.

On these days Alison takes Julie back to her own apartment, where Julie refuses the big mug of sweet peppermint tea and grilled cheese and tomato sandwiches that Alison cuts into fingers. She rubs Julie's back, munching bits of neglected sandwich, as Julie rocks back and forth on her couch, heaving animal sobs into her throw blanket. Alison chews quickly and feels terrible for being so happy that Julie isn't pregnant. For being so happy they can both still get drunk on Strawberry Angel, which stains their tongues brilliant ruby. Alison stumbling home in the dark to sit on the balcony and watch the pink house, waiting for something to happen. One of these nights a man in a blue ski jacket chases another man down the street, punches him in the head before he scrambles inside the door to his apartment building. Heart pounding, Alison goes inside and jots down the particulars on an empty Crunch 'n Munch box, in case she has to call the police or be interviewed by CFRN. The blue ski jacket man rattles the glass door for half an hour, occasionally putting his hands in his pockets and throwing his whole body against the door. Alison crouches inside by her patio doors, licking her fingertips and pressing them into crushed bits of caramel corn and peanuts at the bottom of the box. The man finally gives up, speeds away in his grey Oldsmobile (or Alison passes out and dreams this, she's not sure which). She sleeps on her apartment floor, hugging the Crunch 'n Munch box. She wakes the next morning when her neighbour slams a door. Her sweaty hands have smudged the notes off the box. Alison tells Julie about the episode and how she can no longer mix Crunch 'n Munch (at least not the kind with peanuts) with booze because the combination makes her sick to her stomach.

After lunch, Alison attends a Communications Planning course at the Public Affairs Bureau. The same building that houses the Budget Surplus Call Centre, which Alison volunteered for last week, spending four evenings drinking mugs of burned coffee and carefully noting other people's desires. She is the first one in the reception area today, where she waits for Shelley from Food Services to wheel supplies and refreshments into the boardroom. She crosses and recrosses her legs, wishing she'd remembered to double-check the start time. Alison has learned that arriving early is only advisable when you know what you are doing. Arriving early when you don't makes you seem eager or pathetic, which is how she feels as Shelley smiles at her and says, "At least you get first pick of muffins."

A musky-smelling man sits beside Alison, so close she could rest her head on his shoulder, she thinks (and what would happen if she did?). Alison tries to look busy as other people enter the room, running through her grocery list in her new dayplanner— Corn Flakes, Cajun-flavoured Tater Tots, shrimp-flavoured Ichiban, iceberg lettuce, pickled onions, macaroni and cheese, *People Magazine*, seasoning salt and two bags of Bugles. The musky man relaxes in his chair, leans even closer to her. Alison thinks this type of situation is a sick game the universe is playing with her. Tempting her to do the inappropriate. Like when she sits on the bus with people's bums in her face, wanting to goose them. She once yelled, "Boo!" to a homeless man sleeping in a bus shelter. She didn't see him at first and actually meant to shout, "Jesus Christ," or "Holy hell," but *boo* just slipped out. He woke, laughing as she hurried to the next bus stop, ignoring his pleas, "Hey, crazy, come back."

The boardroom lights dim, the overhead projector clicks on and the man beside her rests his head on the boardroom table. Somewhere between PROGRAM GOALS and TARGET AUDIENCE, he starts to snore. Alison looks around, worried that her proximity implicates her in his laziness. To compensate, she jots notes furiously, including all the *ands* and *buts* (the sort of notes she'll look at tomorrow with surprise, and marvel at how she could have been conscious enough to transcribe another person's words, yet distracted enough for the meaning not to have registered).

Alison met Julie at an Internet 101 course. They were seated beside each other in the Training Centre, a windowless boardroom with ten computers and a dining cart with a large carafe of coffee and Styrofoam cups. "I heard people have tons of sex on this," Julie whispered to Alison during the instructor's description of search engines. It took Alison a moment to realize Julie meant the Internet, not the desk. Julie told Alison during the coffee break that she wasn't planning to be an administrative assistant forever. "I figure I'll get out before the carpal tunnel syndrome." Alison nodded thoughtfully and picked at a Boston cream. Julie invited Alison back to her house at the end of the session to hear her sing, which she said was her true calling. Alison accepted, thrilled at the possibility of missing another evening of cruising the aisles of London Drugs for ripple chips and hair dye, wondering if she should get a second job there to fill her nights.

Alison stops at Hull's Foods on her way home from the Communications Planning course. She shops here almost every day. She can't shop the way she used to in Calgary when George would lend her his Bronco. She tells herself that she is now following a more European model, only shopping for what she needs, cooking each day with fresh vegetables and spices (though she buys more Cheemo perogies than kale or broccoli). She wishes she had a shopping basket with wheels, like everyone in Europe seems to, instead of her *I ♥ N.Y.* canvas bag. She carries it with the words against her body, so she doesn't look like one of those people who has never travelled anywhere and borrowed the bag from a well-travelled friend.

There is a blue and white dinner set at Hull's that Alison is trying to complete. With each purchase over $75 customers receive a free piece. She has two dinner plates, a salad plate and a cereal bowl, and has her eye on the serving platter, in case she ever has the nerve to throw a dinner party. Today she plans to buy a new laundry basket, which should make her load a little easier, and she has a hankering for brie (which at $8.99 a wheel should bring her grocery bill to $75). She is already deciding what she will serve herself on her new platter. She might put her whole meal on it, use it as an oversized plate like in the fancy restaurants she and George used to go to.

Alison sets her table for dinner every night with the Mexican print tablecloth she bought at Fields (her apartment came furnished and she covers the table so she doesn't have to look at the word *Nippled* that some prior tenant gouged into it with what looks like a fork). Some days she thinks about taking an axe to the table instead, so she can warm herself with a roaring bonfire on her balcony. She places a magnolia-scented candle in the middle of the table to ward off any old smells that might be reactivated with the heat of her cooking. Occasionally, she shuts the phone off when she eats (though she knows that some guy from the *Edmonton Journal*'s sales department is probably the only one who will call. Sometimes she wishes she had the guts to say, "I'm no longer giving interviews to the press," when the guy says, "Good evening, Ma'am. This is Gerry calling from the *Journal*."). She eats in silence, except for the scrape of her knife and fork and the fake cough that sneaks out when she is nervous or can't think of anything to say. Her apartment looks almost cozy in the candlelight, she can barely see the thin strings of dust that hang from the ceiling and wag like disapproving fingers when the heat unpredictably comes on.

Alison doesn't look at her apartment too critically. When she first moved in, she did a thorough clean, found a half-used tube of Preparation-H lodged between the cushions of the couch and a sticky shooter glass in the closet. She vacuumed the cushions and carpet, scrubbed the floors and walls and vowed to keep the lights low. She bought wooden picture frames, painted them silver and filled them with blank greeting cards. Black and white pictures of Paris and New York. She hung them over nail marks and spots on the wall that wouldn't come clean. She follows Julie's formula for happy living in furnished apartments: "Never look under the bed or behind the fridge."

Alison had supper at Julie's house a week ago. Julie sat crosslegged on a homemade beanbag chair in her living room, performing covers of Hole. Alison watched from the edge of the unmade hide-a-bed, tapping her toe as best she could to the tune, unsure if it was impolite to look around or slip away to the bathroom. She figured Julie might not even notice. She was in a trance, eyes shut, screaming at the top of her lungs. After her music set, Julie made spaghetti tossed in Thousand Island dressing (her own culinary invention) and Alison finally went to the bathroom. She looked through Julie's bathroom cupboard, sniffing vanilla-scented talcum powder and rubbing lotion on her dry elbows, surprised how empty Julie's cabinet was compared to her own—with its half-used shampoos promising shine and volume, hair-removal cream that burns more than it removes and organic hairspray that doesn't hold her hair well and smells of patchouli. Alison smeared some of Julie's Passionberry lip gloss on her lips, rubbing it off with a tissue when she saw her shiny mouth in the mirror. Over supper Julie told Alison that Robbie is getting excited about the possibility of a baby— she doesn't need Alison to come to her doctor's appointments from now on. "I mean, thanks for coming," Julie said, stuffing a forkful of pasta in her mouth, "but it was kind of weird, right?" Alison flushed red, wiped her napkin across her mouth and agreed. Julie drove her home on her way to pick up Robbie from his job at the coffee shop, promising her they'd go sometime for free lattes and blueberry pie. Alison wonders if they ever will. And if they'll ever go to Julie's house when Robbie is home. This makes Alison fantasize that there *is* no Robbie and she is Julie's only friend.

There is a homeless man in a filthy trench coat milling about Hull's produce section, talking to himself, eyeing bananas and cantaloupes and popping the occasional grape into his mouth. It looks like a woman's coat, slim at the waist with the belt tied in a bow behind his back. She wonders if he even knows it is there. She feels embarrassed for him, the way she feels embarrassed for people with toilet paper on their shoe walking confidently through Eaton's Centre after work, imagining that everyone's looking at their smart clothes. Once she followed a woman for fifteen minutes, discreetly trying to step on the paper while she looked through the sales rack of cardigans at Fairweather. She knows it would have been easier to whisper *toilet paper*, or simply point at the woman's shoe. But lately Alison has had the vague notion that she is more awkward than usual and that it might be more embarrassing if the woman *didn't* hear her and it looked as though she was talking to herself in the middle of the mall. She tries not to make eye contact with the homeless man as she bags a head of iceberg lettuce. She hopes he will leave the store before the produce manager shoos him out the front like an alley cat.

Alison imagines her mother will call around suppertime. She left a message for Alison yesterday, concerned she hadn't heard from her. Alison knows she will listen to her mother talk about her father's gastritis, how she has him drinking eight ounces of concentrated aloe juice. She will ask Alison if she wants her to bring aloe or carrot juice when she comes to visit next month. Alison will say, "Whatever you like," as she sucks the seasoning off her All-Dressed Ruffles. Alison will tell her mother she is taking good care of herself. She will stare at the pink house across the road where a plastic bag or a flyer has frozen into a snowdrift in the backyard. She will listen as her mother describes the Qi Gong class she is taking to achieve self-awareness. Alison hopes George will call when she's on the phone with her mother, give up when he hears a busy signal, deciding she's talking to some great new Edmonton boyfriend.

The produce-eating homeless man is the same one from the bus shelter (at least Alison thinks it's the same one). She saw him before, weeks ago, in the household items aisle. She was holding a red shopping basket filled with two bowls, the ones with a recipe for French onion soup printed on the front, and a set of four drinking glasses that look like Mason jars. He was wearing a navy blue blazer with the collar torn off and a T-shirt with a dog on the front that rode up his scrawny stomach. Alison followed him out of the store that day, stopping to adjust her boots each time he looked around. She bunched a ten-dollar bill in her hand, intending to walk up to him and say, "Here you go—gorge yourself on fruit." Instead she turned down an alley, thinking she would beat him to the next corner where she would leave the ten-dollar bill on the ground for him to find. She pulled her shopping bags to her elbows and ran through the snow, but when she reached the next block she saw him walking in the other direction.

The homeless man warms himself on the heating vent behind the checkouts, ignoring the store manager who pulls him to his feet by his collar. Alison feels guilty for pretending to read a newspaper as the man is dragged onto the street, shouting, "String beans." She stuffs her hands in her mittens and wraps her scarf around her mouth, packs up her new laundry basket full of groceries for the walk home. As she turns the corner past Earls, she sees the homeless man sitting on the icy sidewalk. He looks at Alison and says, "What's wrong with you?" wiping his hand across his mouth.

Alison cradles the laundry basket of groceries in front of her and moves down the street. She rocks her basket as she walks and decides that even if the heat is off when she arrives home, she'll make herself a platter full of food. Vegetable spring rolls, cheddar perogies, creamed corn and macaroni and cheese—not the cheap powdered stuff, the good kind with Velveeta.

LIMBO

ABUELA PRETENDS TO NAP. SHE FLUTTERS HER EYELIDS OCCASIONALLY. Monitoring my progress as I unpack my suitcase.

I ask, "Where did Auntie get the new rug?"

"From pirates," she says, eyes shut.

"Pirates, ah yes."

"You listen," her eyes now slightly open in the glare she saves for noisy children and dogs, "buying things from *la policía*—that's no good."

"It's called a police auction. Besides, I bought these at a regular store." I wave a pair of shorts in her direction. "Completely legal."

"*Bueno*." She closes her eyes again. "I sleep now. You stay here."

"I'm not going anywhere." I spread my clothes out on the bed, counting—three tank tops, four T-shirts, three pairs of shorts, seven pairs of panties, one purple sundress and a black dress I quickly stuff under the pile. I put the clothes into the three bottom drawers that Abuela's housekeeper Gracie cleared for me.

"Not enough," Abuela says, her eyes closed.

The last time I saw Abuela, she was mobile. Still cooking, but forgetting goatfish in the oven, charring it into black heaps that crumbled when someone finally scraped it into the garbage. She talked to me for hours about neighbours. Her favourite stories involving death, marriage and moving home, which she has been begging me to do for years—lucky Mrs. Carey whose daughter and grandson moved home after the divorce, stubborn Brian Pyfrom who went to Oxford and married an English girl with red hair, poor Verna Wells whose husband was sent to prison on gambling charges—leaving her with no man and, more importantly, no house.

Lately, she talks more about the past than the present. Her long-dead brothers and my Grandpappy. I bring Abuela gifts every time I visit: small pink soaps and magnolia-scented perfume. She will forget I've brought them and ask, "Who this belong to?" Or reprimand me, "Waste of money—I'm too old for nonsense."

I tell her, "You don't want to smell like old lady, do you?" spraying her neck and wrists as she holds her breath.

— Are you going because you think she's going to die?

— I'm going because I want her to remember me.

— You see her every year—you see her more than I see my grandmother and *she* lives in Saskatchewan.

— It's not the same. She's my last one.

I walk out Abuela's front gate with a faded blue towel and *House and Home* magazine tucked under my arm. It's early enough to slip past the neighbour's big dogs asleep behind their low stone wall. Across the road is my stretch of sand, an inlet at the end of a string of pink and purple hotels. "Why go to such a lonely beach?" Gracie asks. "Down the way there—plenty people." She motions to the hotels. Gracie insists on walking to the end of the road with me each day, Abuela's idea, I soon realize. "You grammy be much happier if you go *dat* way."

"Tell her I'm going to the straw market to buy T-shirts," I say. But Gracie follows me out the gate, still peeling a potato—insisting it is part of her job. I can expect to find Abuela at home, worrying a tissue to shreds, waiting to hear the latch on the iron gate and me shouting, *I'm home*, as I knock on the louvred glass windows beside the front door. "The sea will eat you. Come—stay," she'll say and smack the couch beside her.

As a child I wasn't allowed to go to the beach alone. Even now I imagine I might be punished for wading through clumps of seaweed, eyeing points on the horizon to swim to. I wrap my beach towel around my back, surprised at the coolness of the breeze. I step onto the edge of a rock, brush sand off my feet and slip into sandals before climbing the embankment to the main road. The ocean is colder than I expected. Mangoes aren't even in season. I bought one the other day at the grocer's, but it was imported from California. As I walked back to Abuela's house, the juice dripped like a faucet from the end of my soaked chin onto my T-shirt. "Terrible stain if you no wash right away," she said, wheeling through the doorway. I know these stains—brownish-yellow ones from my childhood, ugly and impenetrable. I picture them on pink shorts, cream terry-cloth jumpsuits and white church blouses with ruffled collars. Abuela sucking her lips across her teeth in disgust at me ruining another outfit. "*Cuidado*," she'd say and pass me the thick mango seed, "hold tight." But my fingers were small and less certain than hers.

— How do you say *shoes* in Spanish?

— *Zapatos.*

— Hug?

— *Abrazo.*

— Empty?

— *Solo.* No, that's *alone.* God, I can't remember. You see what's happening.

— Honey, it's no big deal.

— Maybe to you.

"*Levantate hija,*" she says as she sits on the edge of her bed, kicking my air mattress. She wants me to help her to the bathroom. She hikes her pink nightie up and wraps her arms around my middle. I lower her onto the toilet, amid shouts of, "Oh, Lordy, *gracias.*" Most days I wake quietly, it takes me a few moments to realize where I am, to decide no, I am not dreaming. I collect small details: the cedar blanket box Abuela now uses for old dresses (the ones with holes that she is nevertheless reluctant to throw away), the silver relief picture of Jesus she insisted on taking to the hospital for her operation (just in case), the comforting huff and puff of her laboured breathing.

"What about this one?" I yawn and hold up a blue dress with a delicate white collar. A dress I have seen her wear in photographs from before I was born. I have just finished giving her a sponge bath. A chore both of us hate. Her refusing to make eye contact as I drag a soapy cloth across her thighs, dipping quickly between them. As a child I never saw Abuela naked, believing she bathed in the black bra and slip I so often saw her in. The thin straps embedded into her fleshy shoulders seemed to be part of her.

She looks at the blue dress, "I not know who that belong to."

"You," I say as I unzip the dress and slip it off the hanger.

"No," she says. She fixes her eyes on the ceiling and does not move. It's a warm day so I powdered her after her bath, hoping to stop the spread of the heat rash that peppers her body. She looks like a powdered doughnut, the swell of her belly holding extra talc like a mountain.

"Come." I swing her legs around the side of the bed. I put on her underwear, bra and slip. She pushes herself off the bed.

"I no remember." The insistence is gone from her voice and she looks me in the eye. And I have to look away. I slip the dress over her head and smooth it down the sides of her body. It fits perfectly. Standing in front of the mirror, she looks at herself. "Well, apparently the dress remembers you," I say, resting my hand in the small of her back where the dress sits snugly.

After breakfast I move Abuela to the couch where she likes to lie, propped up on fat cushions, looking out the front window at the street. The few times I have decided to try something different and sit her outside in a folding chair, she starts kicking the door with her good foot, shouting, "*Hija*, take me from here. I too hot." I help her into her chair and wheel her back inside. "You stick me out there to bake—you know what I call you—*Sin verguenza*." She relaxes on the couch and loosens her tight forehead when I ask whether she would like an extra pillow, a cup of lemon tea. I know she is losing her memory—that her mind is disintegrating like a hard cookie in warm milk. But some days I think she is just too stubborn to remember. When details like my name or whether I'm her child or grandchild seem less important than the weeds she ate during the civil war (*puerros*), the colour she was wearing the day her own mother died (red).

I ask, "Where did you meet Pappy?" pulling the ottoman close to the couch.

"In España—we both worked for a family."

"You were the maid, yes?"

"No, *la dama de companía*—how do you say?"

"Lady in waiting," I smile. "Yes, you were the lady in waiting. And Pappy?"

She pauses, fixes her eyes on the curtains or the road outside.

"He was the help for their boy," she says, clasping her hands over her chest.

"Did they only have one son?"

"Yes, I believe so—I don't know." She is quiet again.

"It's okay," I say, "tell me about the day you met Pappy. Was he the darkest man you'd ever seen? Was he handsome?"

She pauses, looks past her slippered feet and out the window. "I thought I would marry from my village. Barros—the north of Spain," she says. "Money was bad. I went to work. I had no choice. Now see me." She looks right at me now. "I move to another country. My husband is dead. This is how it happens." She shakes her head, bites her bottom lip.

"Were you scared?" I ask, settling onto the couch beside her. "Did you want to move?" She closes her eyes and pauses so long I think she is asleep.

"On the boat I lie down all day—" she stops, again. "And *por la noche,* I come out when people sleep to throw up all down the side. Two weeks to get to this place. Every day I say *Dios mio,* I pray, *Dios te salve María llena eres de gracia, el Señor es con tigo....*" She makes the sign of the cross over her lips and then mine. "This is how it happens," she says.

I rest my head close to hers. She doesn't shoo me away like she usually does, claiming she can't sleep with someone too close to her face. I look up at her. This woman who is neither adventurous nor romantic. This woman who left her home to follow a man across the ocean to a place she had never been with a tiny baby and all of her family's warnings ringing in her ears.

I whisper, "How could you ever love someone that much?"

"Love?" she says sleepily, as though it is the first time she has heard the word.

She is quiet. And I remember the story. How she slept beside him all night long, knowing he was dead, but not wanting it to be true until morning.

I am running past thick royal palms, pink oleander trees, and iron gates with ceramic nameplates that read *Androsia House, Blue Marlin, Sea Grape Manor* and *Fire Coral*. My usual jog takes me around the corner past Dicky Mo's bar and onto the manicured pathway that curls past the Cable Beach hotels, thick with the smell of jasmine at night. Today, I am running in the other direction, away from the ocean and past Abuela's neighbours, whose comings and goings she watches through her front window. I turn right and should eventually reach City Meat Market or Cole Thompson's pharmacy where I'll stop for a bottle of water before making my way back. But the sun is high, almost white, and it bleaches the road. Little grey dots float through my field of vision, they fall like deflating balloons. I close my eyes, run my hand over my sweaty forehead. I know where I am, I tell myself. I can only be a few streets away from Abuela's house.

The pharmacy door jingles as I enter. I stand for a moment in the entryway under the icy blast of air conditioning. Next to the door sit four racks of postcards, local landmarks and scenes photographed through heavy filters, one dollar apiece. I buy the same ones every trip. Fort Charlotte, the straw market, Queen's Staircase and the water tower, the last place my father took me before we moved off the island. It was there that he told me we were moving to Canada, lifting me onto his shoulders and pointing me in the right direction. From the water tower, the island seems small and uncomplicated. You can see the ocean to the north and to the south. I finger the thick cardboard and decide to buy another. The kind of party scene I usually avoid: a beach sunset, a dancing crowd, a flaming limbo stick. I have started writing postcards, describing the colour of the sky (*cerulean*, a word I picked more for its sound than its accuracy), which fruits are in season (grapefruit, oranges, lemons and jujus), which hotels have been built or rebuilt (the British Colonial is back to its original glory and its original colour), how the wind cracked the royal palm in the front yard last week (narrowly missed the neighbour's cat). I read them over and tuck them away, hoping tomorrow to move past the scenery. At the pharmacy cash desk I buy a large bottle of water and a tube of rose-scented hand lotion for Abuela. I hook the small plastic bag around my wrist and walk past the yellow post office.

"Where were you?" my husband asks into the phone. "What were you doing? Your Abuela was worried."

I fiddle with my bottle of water. "I was running."

"Where?"

"God, why does it matter?" I peel my hot leg off the plastic kitchen stool.

"Look, she was concerned," he says. "So was I."

"She's calling me," I say. "I'm all right, okay? I'll call you soon."

I wheel Abuela's empty wheelchair around to the couch where she lies staring at the ceiling. I settle into the folds of the plastic seat. I lean over to kiss her, tell her that I'm sorry, I got lost, but she reaches out and pinches my cheek. "*Eres estúpida,*" she says, averting her eyes. "*Solo piensa en lo que tu quieres.*" I roll my eyes and push back from the couch. "*Cuidado, te vas ha hacer daño*—you could fall and someone takes you away like that. Stay in *la casa*—stay." I wait until she falls asleep before going to shower.

I stand in the stream of the cool water and think about calling my husband back, about whether to return to my usual routine. How many times can I cover the same ground? I turn toward the shower stream and let water break over my face. Shampoo foams down my back. Water rushes into my mouth, I gasp and splutter, but do not turn away. I slick my hand over my hair and grab my stomach, unsettled from the run and the heat.

"*¿Estas casada?*" Abuela asks, slipping my wedding band up and down my finger. We are in the kitchen. She is soaking her feet in a basin of water, softening them before I clip her toenails. I move my chair in front of her and spread a towel across my legs.

"Remember the wedding? You wore the pink dress, the one with the pearl buttons?" She drops my hand and I pull her left foot from the water into my lap.

"He is a good man?"

"Yes—you remember." I clip the thick nail on her big toe, careful not to cut too deep. The nail falls in long splinters into the basin and floats on the surface.

"You here all by yourself," she says, as if she has just considered this for the first time. "When my husband was here, I go nowhere without him. You girls take too many *libertades.*" I dry her foot and calf, careful not to pull her papery skin.

"It is no longer considered indecent for a married woman to travel without her husband," I say, pulling her right foot out of the water.

"So you say." She examines her fingers, waiting for me to offer to clip them next. "When I move here with my husband, I no speak a word—I want to go home—but this is my life," she says.

"I know," I say, taking her hand.

She touches my wedding ring again. "Who you belong to?" she says, in a voice so strong and clear it belies her forgetfulness. I am quiet for a moment. And before I can answer she changes direction, "Where is *la música?*"

In the kitchen we listen to Abuela's Cuban station. She doesn't watch satellite TV anymore, not even the Argentinean channels. She says their South American accents annoy her— the hard Cs, the nasal Ns. "That," she says as she rolls her eyes, "is not *Español.*" These subtleties I hardly hear, the people on the TV talk so quickly I take away only the familiar words. *Mejor. Calor. Frío.* Abuela speaks and I know her language through context, the way she moves her eyes and the way she tells the same story over and over again.

I sit on a Bowe's island jitney packed with tourists. The windows are open and there is the smell of salt air mixed with gas, the cry of cicadas in the grass. Little breeze can make it past the bulk of bodies, many in bright bikini tops and shorts, holding the loops of plastic that hang from the ceiling. Sweat drips down their faces, settles in the folds of skin at their shoulders. The reggae station up full blast so conversations turn to shouting about whether to eat lunch again at Conch Fritters. Whether to visit the slave museum or the pirate museum. Whether Butler & Sands is the cheapest place to buy rum. Whether or not there is a limbo party on the beach tonight. A woman with tiny plaits in her light brown hair sings loudly to the music, though she doesn't know the words. The driver smiles at her, honks his horn in appreciation. The jitney stops by the British Colonial on West Bay, a few blocks down from the straw market. I pass the stalls that spill onto the street— tables of pink and black coral necklaces and earrings, shellacked wooden beer mugs with oversized handles, cheap T-shirts with iron-on decals of Bahamian flags or fat bottles of Kalik Gold beer. The women beckon, shouting, "Come here, sweet thing," and, "Look here, child, I have what you need." I consider the colourful batik sarongs, and straw change purses, beach bags and hats, all embroidered with flowers or names in fuchsia, teal and canary yellow, but I continue walking.

In line at the bank, I think about going back. I wonder if I should brave the crowds and buy the green sarong with the yellow edge. I'd use it here, but back home it would sit in a drawer. I finally hear the teller calling me and when I get up to the wicket she says, "You okay, Ma'am? You look lost."

— How's it going?

 — It's just not the same.

 — What isn't?

 — The palm trees—they cut the trees in the front yard.

 — I only saw the yard once. I probably wouldn't notice the difference.

 — You probably wouldn't. But I miss those trees.

 — I miss you.

 — I miss you too.

 — More than the trees?

"A change of scenery," I say as Abuela shifts her weight towards me and I lower her into the passenger seat. I fold the wheelchair and place it in the trunk of the car. "We need a fresh perspective," I say and grab her hand as I buckle her seat belt. "Compass Point," I smile, "you can eat fried grouper and plantain and coleslaw—anything you want." We drive onto Bay Street heading west, past the food store and the pink and yellow apartment towers that blaze in the midday sun. The road narrows and the asphalt looks wet at the edges as if sunlight is melting everything away.

We park across the street in a gravel lot. Terrain we must negotiate carefully. I move Abuela into her wheelchair and roll it down the makeshift path of plywood pieces from the neighbouring construction site. From the front, the building is unassuming; heavy foliage hangs around the simple stone arch of a doorway. Inside, the colours turn hot: yellow walls, red and orange tables, bright blue doors leading to the kitchen and bathrooms. We are shown to a dark mauve table on the violet balcony that overlooks the ocean. The seawall is salmon pink and lined with dozens of shiny pink conch shells. I position Abuela so she can watch the people in the restaurant and I can watch the water. The waiter sets large glasses of lemon iced tea on pink napkins. The glasses sweat in the heat. "This is nice," I say, stirring spoonfuls of sugar into my drink.

"I suppose," says Abuela, scanning the balcony for the waiter. "You get the man to bring me my fish," she says. "Don't forget *platano*."

Most days we eat our lunch on TV trays so Abuela doesn't have to move from her couch. I try to convince her to come to the table, for us to eat lunch on full-sized plates instead of the small ones that fit better on the stackable tables. But she says that as soon as she's manoeuvred to the big table, it's time to move back and just not worth the effort anymore. I set up the trays and help Gracie serve her simple lunches like boiled fish with rice and carrots. I eat peanut butter and jam and she tries to grab it out of my hands and shouts, "*¡Da me lo!*" until I give her a bite. She turns back to her food in disgust. "This food is fit for the dead."

She eats her fried fish in silence. The occasional "mmm mmm." I promised her she could have whatever she wanted today, including dessert, and I wouldn't tell her nurse. Her blood sugar reading tomorrow will give us both away, but for now we sit, imagining the sticky guava duff with rum and butter sauce that we will order when the waiter comes to clear our dishes. We will deal with the consequences later.

— Why didn't you move back?
  — I met you.
  — And now you wish you could go back?
  — I never said that.
  — So what *are* you saying?
  — Nothing—stop reading into everything.
  — Okay, fine. When are you coming home?

"*Ponme mis pendientes,*" Abuela says, holding her pearl earrings in her left hand. She shuffles her feet along the floor, pulling her wheelchair closer to where I'm sitting on the bed.

My ears were pierced when I was three days old. Abuela did it. My father couldn't watch, couldn't stay in the house. He walked out the back door as my mother scooped me from my bassinet on the kitchen table and held me over the counter. Abuela, boiling her best sewing needles in a small pot of water on the stove, swabbed my tiny earlobes with alcohol.

"How did you pierce my ears?"

"A potato, a needle and *un cubito de hielo,*" she says. "*Ponme mis pendientes.*"

Abuela is waiting. Her left earring hole has grown over and I will have to push the stem of her pearl earring through the scar tissue. I am hoping she will forget in a moment that she has asked me at all.

She is insistent. "You no need *la patata. De prisa.*" Abuela takes the earring and scratches it against the lobe of her ear, drilling for a hole. I take the earring out of her hand.

"Stop. I'll do it."

She tells me how she rubbed ice cubes over my ears until they were numb, pinching them to see if I flinched. Held a small piece of raw potato behind my tiny lobe and stabbed the needle through the flesh.

"No blood," she says, bobbing her head in a satisfied nod.

"Did I cry?"

She doesn't answer me.

Her ear is soft and elastic, stretching like bread dough as I pull. I press the flesh between my thumb and middle finger, feeling the hard pebble of tissue where the hole used to be.

"*Ahora,*" Abuela says, grabbing my hand.

"Wait," I say, moving the lamp closer. I turn the lobe over, examining it closely for even the tiniest sliver of light to show me a way out. Her ear glows red and I sit back down on the bed. "I don't think I can do it," I say. "Not like you."

"You are *un cobarde*," she says, grabbing the pearl again. "*Ponlo*." She waves it in front of my face.

"Jesus Christ, okay." My hands are trembling now. "Why is this so important now? Where are you going? It's been grown over for years."

She sighs and fixes her eyes on the wall in front of her. I place my thumb behind the lobe and position the earring with my other hand.

"*Uno, dos, tres, cuatro . . .*" Abuela counts, not looking at me.

I press the earring, not stopping against the resistance. Her flesh stretches and stretches under my pressure. I move my thumb for a moment and look at the underside of her lobe, forming a rounded bulge that looks like the head of a penis, the eye fused shut.

"*Siete, ocho, nueve . . .*"

With one last push the blunt earring stem punctures my thumb. We both inhale sharply. I suck my thumb hard and she bites her lip. The pearl is pink with blood. We look at each other, not wanting to be the first to cry.

— Do you ever wish you were sick?
   — Sure. I could use a catch-up day.
   — I mean really sick.
   — Is everything okay there?
   — Yes, fine.
   — You mean those days in bed with tissues and soup?
   — When your biggest decision is *Regis* or *Maury*.

I sit on Abuela's back porch, drinking rum and ginger ale, my husband's favourite, and watch the light as it fades in the back-yard. The pear and sugar banana trees lit up by the battery-operated garden lights I installed for her yesterday. Laughter rises from the nearby hotels, the guests preparing for the evening, pouring into restaurants and poolside bars. I go inside when my aunt arrives and help her move Abuela, who has fallen asleep on the couch. Her body is heavy and warm, I hold her a long moment before lowering her into her wheelchair and then her bed. "You going?" she mumbles, eyes still closed. I stand over her for a while, stroking her thin white hair.

I walk with my drink to my small beach, over the rocks and up the sand until I reach the hotels. I sit on a plastic beach lounger and watch the hotel guests drink and dance on a patio encircled with tiny paper lanterns. People having fun, people on vacation. There are jugs of strawberry and lime daiquiri on every table, big bouquets of pink and white frangipani, women in silver dress sandals with pink sunburn lines across their backs, men in linen pants and tasselled shoes without socks. They sway to the calypso band as they wait their turn in the limbo line. I smile as they contort their bodies, bending too early or too late, legs too close together, stumbling into the broomstick held between two hotel employees dressed in white shorts and navy-collar shirts. One man falls on his back, a roar of laughter goes up as he recovers, crawls under the bar on all fours. A young woman almost makes it, then pauses under the bar, her feet unsteady, and she collapses, shaking her head in disappointment.

Abuela is about to limbo. She pulls her blue and white dress to the middle of her eighty-year-old thighs with one hand and leans back slightly as she approaches the burning stick. She shakes her shoulders side to side. Bends her knees, spreads her legs wide and tilts her pelvis. Her eyes are shut and the veins in her long neck jut out as she throws her head back and shimmies—thighs, crotch, belly, ribs, breasts, collarbone—below flame as her dusty feet shuffle along the white tile floor. There is a moment when she hovers and I wonder if she'll make it, but she jumps up on the other side and screams with delight, touching her hands to her damp chest, tugging at her polyester dress.

She grabs the young woman's hand and pulls her close and the two of them spin, knocking into tables and chairs.

Neither one of us wants to let go.

ALEGRÍA

━━

THE BOAT GLIDES FORWARD, THEN TUGS BACK. HELD SECURELY IN place by the silt-covered anchor. Anthony lies awake below in the berth, arms crossed over his chest.

Sara stands naked in the cramped head, legs shoulder-width apart, trying to keep her balance. She splashes tepid water over her face and brushes her teeth. Her elbows knock the walls with each wave that breaks against the boat. She has a purple bruise on her arm from when she tripped entering the cabin and launched herself into the chest of drawers. "Jesus Christ," she shouted then, and now around a mouthful of toothbrush as she kicks her foot against the wooden floor.

Anthony opens his eyes, whispers, "Serves you right," into the dark, salty air. The boat is still for a brief moment. Sara rubs a wet hand across her open mouth and clutches her stomach. She dries her face on the same frayed green towel she and

Anthony have been sharing for the past three days. Her towel is in the black duffle bag Anthony forgot to load on the boat in Nassau. They are sailing between Out Islands. Sara's friend, who grew up in the Bahamas, told them to stay away from the capital if they wanted to escape the booze cruise crowd.

Sara stares into the mirror past her pale arms and sunburned cheeks and listens. The talking and giggling behind the wall have subsided. Past the leaky toilet that squirts water into her eyes each time she pumps the handle to flush and the medicine cabinet that creaks on its loose hinges is a second cramped cabin, identical to Anthony and Sara's—only reversed. The same berth and water-stained mattress consuming much of the cabin, the same chest of drawers requiring such effort to open that they lie empty—bags at the foot of the bed, the same small porthole beside the bed, looking onto the starboard deck and hatch from which the now-gathered sails are visible.

Sara rejected the second room because it was noisier, too close to the generator, its constant hum that has become the soundtrack to each evening's activities. She has strained all weekend to make out the words and noises behind that wall. She sighs, runs her hands through her recently cut hair, a style Anthony calls severe, and opens the bathroom door. "Jesus Christ," Anthony says in a loud whisper, "I'm trying to sleep here." He shields his eyes.

Sara flicks the light switch, absentmindedly attempts to pull her cropped hair into a ponytail. She shuffles a few steps, stops at the foot of the cot. "Where are you?" she says, waving her arms in front of her, grabbing Anthony's toes. "I can't see you."

He kicks his foot and turns away. Sara pulls herself into bed, the top of her head just missing the low wooden bulkhead above. She settles beside Anthony and fans her hand above her face, a faint breeze from the overhead hatch enters the musty cabin. The day has been hotter than expected, but Anthony is still wearing a blue-collared golf shirt, the one with his company's large yellow emblem that Sara calls tasteless.

"Are you tired?" Sara asks, slipping her hand up the back of his shirt and onto his sticky back.

"Stop—" He bristles, turns towards the small, circular port-holes on the cabin wall and pulls the thin cotton sheet over his shoulder.

"Fine," she grabs her flat pillow, folds it in half before flop-ping her head down. "You're making a big deal out of noth-ing," she says and watches his round shoulder rising out of the darkness.

"Drop it," he says, flips onto his back and speaks into the low bulkhead. His voice echoes back towards them.

"Look—" she pauses, huffs out a hot blast of air. "What are you so angry about?" She sits up and bumps her forehead on the ceiling. "Shit."

"For Christsake, keep it down. They've heard enough out of you tonight," he says.

"God, I can't believe you're still ticked off about *that*. We were just kidding around," Sara says, shaking her head, then massages her temples with the heels of her hands.

"Kidding around," Anthony repeats crisply like he is repeat-ing back a phone number or giving directions to their new house. "Leave me alone," he says and grabs the top of Sara's arm.

"Let go of me *now*." She wiggles her arm free, slides to the end of the bed and slips her legs over the edge, bashing her heels into the high baseboard that stops just below the mattress. *Thump. Thump. Thump.*

Anthony is silent.

The boat shifts and Sara climbs back towards him. "Anthony, come on." She lies on her side facing him, exhales a long breath, reaches her hand beneath the sheet and drags her fingers over his stomach, then under the tight elastic on his blue and white plaid boxer shorts.

"Screw off." He bats her hand away, presses his shoulder against the wall.

"I thought maybe—"

Anthony rolls over, his hands balled up into tight fists. "The problem is you never think."

He shakes his head and presses his cheek against the port-hole. Sara looks at him, watches the fading horizon bob up and down over the edge of the boat.

Michael sits on top of Jill and peppers her bare chest with kisses. She grabs his head with both her hands, bites the lobe of his left ear playfully. "Ouch," he says, "so that's the way it's going to be?" He takes a deep breath and holds it for a moment, then blows it out with his lips pressed against Jill's tight brown stomach. She giggles, pulls him towards her and kisses him on the mouth.

She asks, "Shouldn't you be manning the deck, Captain?"

"You see, matey," he mumbles, his face buried in her chest, "when you've been at sea as long as I have. . . ." He slides his hands down her legs, raises her short yellow skirt and smacks her behind.

Jill lets out a muffled yelp. "Michael, stop," she says, knocking her head against the low ceiling. "Ouch, shit—we need to be quiet." She rubs her head and pouts her bottom lip.

"Let me see your ouchy," he says, pulling her shoulders back towards the berth. "Is this where it hurts?" He lifts her skirt again, pointing to the purple string bikini bottoms he bought her especially for the trip, the ones he tied around her beach towel and said, "Now all you need is sunglasses."

"Seriously." She stifles a laugh as he traces his fingers up her inner thighs. "You saw how they were at supper." She pulls the elastic from her hair and runs her fingers through it. "Can you believe she said that?"

"What I can't believe is how hard it is to untie these bikini thingies." He uses his teeth, gnaws at the tiny knot. The skin beneath the bikini is as creamy brown as her thighs that shift each time she speaks.

"They're your friends," she says. "Why would she embarrass him like that?" She sits up, ducking her head, pulls her skirt down and shoos Michael's hands away. She settles in front of him and runs her hands over his chest, stopping to finger the thick white scar on his shoulder. When Jill first noticed it, Michael smiled and said it was the result of a passionate lover's quarrel. She later learned it had more to do with beer and barbed wire than love, but she told him she liked it just the same.

"Is she mad about him leaving the bag?" she says, knitting her thin eyebrows together into a tight clump.

Michael smoothes her wrinkled forehead with his thumb. "Okay, we will talk about this for exactly thirty-seconds. Three, two, one, go!" Michael sits cross-legged on the bed, holds an imaginary stopwatch in his hand. "On second thought," he says, his lips curling into a smile Jill calls devilish, "let's go borrow Sara's stopwatch, she's probably through timing poor Tony for the night."

"Jesus," Jill yelps. "Be quiet, they'll hear you." Michael jumps onto the bed, pins her arms to her sides, licks her lips and blows on them. "Yuck," Jill groans, "be serious. We don't want them to think—"

"To think we're actually having fun." He crawls off her. "Okay, Jill, let's have no fun, either, let's get good jobs, buy a starter home and an Aerostar, spend weekends laying sod, and our whole vacation wishing there was a TV and a Blockbuster in the next lagoon." He lies still, closes his eyes and clasps his hands in prayer. "Good night, dear. Got to say my prayers. Our Father who art in Heaven . . ."

Jill rolls on top of him, "Okay, stop it."

"Thy Kingdom come, thy will be . . . sorry, I blacked out for a minute there, what did you say?" He smiles, slipping down to the floor and grabbing her feet. "Are we having fun again? That was scary for a minute, I almost got myself out of the mood."

"Almost?" says Jill as she messes his thick blond hair with her foot.

"It was a close one, I tell you." He takes her silver-polished baby toe into his mouth, "Mmm, salty," he says, talking around it, "I'm hungry." He slips his tongue between each toe, looking at her as he flutters his dark brown eyelashes. Jill stretches out on the bed and flexes her feet like a cat.

"Maybe we should go—" Jill says, pointing to the ceiling.

"For a little deck maintenance." He winks at her. "Yes, Jilly, you must polish the brass handles—buff them harder, harder."

"Shhh, pass me my top." She motions to the wooden floor.

A wave pushes the side of the boat. Michael stumbles reaching for her shirt, falls to the floor. "It's rough, do you like it rough?"

She grabs the shirt, pulls it over her head and says, "I'll show you rough, big fella." She raises her eyebrows and wiggles to the end of the bed, putting a finger to her lips and motioning to the door.

Sara, eyes wide open, listens to the footsteps on the deck above. She glances at Anthony, watches his back rise and fall slowly with each deep breath. It is a side of him she sees so often that she's named constellations in his freckles: Clydesdale horse, baseball pennant, garden trowel, giant Easter egg.

"What do you want me to say?" Sara whispers into Anthony's back as she pulls up close behind him, wrapping her arms around his thick middle.

Anthony pulls her arms off him, pokes her away with his elbows.

"Talk to me." She scratches her head in quick, agitated strokes.

"There is nothing to talk about."

She snorts and turns away. "Jesus, I was kidding."

"You were kidding—" he says, his words precise and awake.

"Look, Anthony, I just want—" she says.

"You just want—" He moves closer to the wall, the worn sheet bunched between them. "You want to take every opportunity to let people know how inadequate you think I am. You think you deserve someone better, someone who knows how to drive a boat, someone who knows what a tiger lily looks like, someone who paints garage doors and toenails too, someone who speaks French and even Spanish, I suppose?" He waits. "You don't realize that someone like that would never want someone like—"

Sara is quiet. The cabin is perfectly still for a minute, the doors pause in their creaking and the lapping water sounds far away. Sara opens her mouth as though she is about to speak. Quiet laughter trails down the open hatch above. She looks at Anthony's back, pulls the sides of her pillow over her ears and wraps her arms over her head.

The room is almost black now. Sara gets out of bed, feels her way along the wall to the head. She sits on the closed toilet and pulls her knees up, tries to rock in time with the boat. She hears Michael shut off the generator for the night. The thick air is suddenly silent. Soon she hears Jill and Michael's voices through the hatch overhead.

"Hey, look, there's another boat out there," says Jill. "I didn't even notice."

"You were busy," Michael says.

"What is it called?" She is quiet, trying to read the name. "*Algebra*? Doesn't sound like a boat name, does it?"

"Mmm, *Algebra*. I had a very sexy math teacher in grade six," Michael says, "thick long hair, much like yours in fact."

"Wait a second, I can't make it out ... *Algeria*?"

"Make out in *Algeria*. That's a nice name, but let's make out here, okay?"

Sara listens to the rhythmic clinking against the boat rail.

"That's not the name, silly." Jill sounds out of breath. "Wait ... one ... minute ..."

"For ... what?"

"The name," she pauses, "just help me figure out the name."

"Okay, where? Ale-gri—" Michael is silent.

Sara runs her hands over her face, gets up, climbs on top of the toilet and braces herself against the wall. She pokes her head as far as she can through the hatch and looks into the darkness. The razor edge of the moon cuts the black sky and she can only see their feet, both facing the railing. Jill on her tiptoes, Michael shifting behind her.

He groans, "*Alegría.*" Then he is silent. The sound of the word fills Sara's eyes with tears, though it is in a language she doesn't understand.

THE PEPPER SMUGGLER

<hr>

THE FIRST MESSAGE ARRIVES ON A TUESDAY WHILE MADELEINE IS sorting through her inbox, deleting old e-mail messages. They hang over her head like dirty clouds. Those nights she can't sleep, thinking about things she hasn't done, needs to do—mistakes she's made.

    Are you there?

It appears in the corner of her monitor, accompanied by a noise that reminds her of the books on tape she listened to as a child. The sound of revelation that told her it was time to turn the page.

    It's me . . . Vinita.

Madeleine fumbles with the mouse. Clicks on the message window to respond. She enters the chatroom.

    Vinita, I'm here. Signing in from Calgary.

    I just added you to my contacts yesterday and now here we are . . .

How's Texas?

I miss Nassau. But I'm learning to drive—again. Sammy doesn't trust my island driving. This is the sprawling metropolis of Cleburne, after all.

How's everything else?

He hardly talks—drives me flipping crazy.

What about a college course?

I can't. I don't have a social security number. I'm here on a spousal visa . . . so I can't be anything but Sammy's wife.

A cooking class?

Madeleine waits but no reply appears. She clicks the message window, wonders if there is a problem with her connection.

At least you married someone you loved.

Madeleine reads this, sits and watches the cursor blink expectantly on the screen. Holds her fingers above the keyboard. She hasn't spoken to Vinita in months, but wants to move past cooking classes and driving lessons. She hesitates at this invitation.

Madeleine and Will received only a formal wedding announcement when Vinita married. And a photograph of the bride and groom on the beach. Vinita in a fuchsia sari, her chocolate-brown eyes lined in kohl. Madeleine was sure she would call. That if it weren't for the short notice or long distance she'd have been invited. Vinita didn't call until weeks later. And Madeleine was surprised when she found herself relieved. Unsure of what to say—*Congratulations*—*what the hell are you doing, agreeing to an arranged marriage?*

Another message pops up before Madeleine can respond.

What am I going to do?

She takes a deep breath.

I'm so sorry.

And she's not sure what for.

I've heard you can take courses on-line. Maybe you could learn a language. Like Spanish. Get your mind off things.

Madeleine winces as she types this, surprised at herself for wanting to continue the safe stream of conversation. She adds, It's totally normal for you not to know if you are in love with Sammy yet. Really, it would be weirder if you were.

He's too Indian. But I guess I've made my bed. Do you know how it feels to have sex with—

Madeleine waits for the end of the sentence that doesn't come. She rubs her forehead.

Jesus Christ, say you have a yeast infection. Then adds, At least until you figure out what you want to do.

Madeleine thinks of how she saw Vinita two months after the wedding, both home in Nassau for Christmas. How she listened to the constant click of Vinita's glass wedding bangles on the coffee table as they flipped through the pages of the wedding album. The afternoon light shone on gold flecks in Vinita's sky-blue sari as she tossed her scarf over her shoulder. Madeleine grabbed a handful of cloth, surprised at its light weight, and said, "You look like a *real* Indian bride." Vinita kissed the red *bindi* sticker she had placed on Madeleine's forehead and they held hands like schoolgirls while eating the generous servings of cauliflower curry and *dal* Vinita's mother set before them. Madeleine whispered: *Has he touched you?*

She hoped for Vinita's sake that Sammy was modest. His parents staying with them in Texas before returning to India. Thin walls. A creaking bed.

A new message. I want to be careful. Let's talk about something else.

Jesus . . . Vinita. What?

Madeleine types quickly. Her foot taps the leg of her desk, thudding her computer monitor against the wall.

I'm breaking out in god-damned hives or something. What do think it could be?

Maybe it's something you ate.

Who knows? I should go. He'll be home soon.

Vinita's icon disappears from the screen. And Madeleine looks out the window. Fills in the details. Conjures up a world for Vinita from bits and pieces of information she receives long distance. Pictures Vinita sitting at her kitchen table in Cleburne, looking out at a stretch of grass perhaps, not unlike her Alberta prairie. She remembers them as young girls driving around Nassau on their lunch breaks from the bank, looking for the trunk lunches Madeleine's mother told her not to eat. Hiking their skirts up to their thighs and licking the grease off their fingers as they listened to Vinita's tapes—the latest Bollywood soundtracks. They'd sit in Vinita's car, the air conditioning on full blast, and gulp down the spicy fish and rice. Inspecting each other's teeth afterward for telltale spices or slivers of food, smelling each other's breath. They were eighteen the summer Madeleine came back to live in the Bahamas after ten years away. Vinita was dating a black boy who worked at the Shell adjacent to the bank. He was a secret. Not Indian and not the kind of boy she would risk being seen with in public. Some lunch hours they would meet him at The Reef restaurant, Madeleine the decoy if any Indians walked in. "Jesus Christ—any brown people?" Vinita whispered as Madeleine scanned the restaurant each time the door jingled open. The boy would laugh, stroking Vinita's shiny black hair as she popped conch fritters into her mouth, looking around like an escaped criminal.

"Beautiful," he said, putting his feet up on the seat in front of him and winking at her. And Madeleine smiled in agreement, wishing she had Vinita's sharp nose, full eyebrows.

Sammy looked the way Vinita imagined. Tall, quiet and neat. His narrow features gave him an air of elegance. Almost condescension. Her mother didn't have a picture to show Vinita before she left, but described him as best she could to Vinta during a phone call with one of Sammy's aunts in India.

Miami was her first stop. On the way to India to meet the candidates. "Your choice entirely," her mother said as Vinita zipped up her suitcase, trying not to tear the delicate sari fabric in the metal teeth.

"As if," Vinita said under her breath. But she knew her mother was right. She was the one who on her eighteenth birthday announced over dinner that she wanted an arranged marriage. "My only request is no one poor or ugly." Her mother laughed so hard she caught a tiny fish bone in her throat, which finally passed when she ate a half loaf of milk-soaked bread.

Ten years later, on her twenty-eighth birthday, Vinita, still unmarried, had an epiphany. She had knocked herself unconscious when she fell off a stepladder while helping her mother hang balloons for her party. When she finally came to, amid screams and cold compresses, she knew what she had to do. Her family would never accept her marrying her Bahamian boyfriend and there were few eligible Indian men on the island to choose from. The time was right and the photos started arriving. Most from cousins and aunties in India, but some from families directly—friends of the family, or strangers who had seen the personal ads Vinita had explicitly asked her mother not to post.

"I'm not a frigging used TV. 'Good colour, good reception. Must go quickly'."

Close-shaven men with starched collars and tight smiles looking out at her, accompanied by taglines (plays chess, knows how to make nice cup of tea) or disclaimers (old photo—has since started cricket, now wonderfully athletic). She lined the photos on her dresser like baseball cards, her equivalent of batting averages and runs-on-base discreetly penned in the upper back corner. DP (definite possibility) and her brother's favourite, NFC (nice fucking chance). She imagined there were pictures of her out there too. Photos her mother had sent without her permission. Flattering ones, she hoped. Taken from the left, her good side. The side that made her look thinner, softened the angle of her nose.

"Sammy?" she said, now approaching the tall Indian man beside the food court.

He stared at her a moment, clearing his throat. "How old are you?"

"Sammy?" she repeated, this time her pitch rising.

"Yes," he said eventually, "I am Sammy. But you look younger than Auntie said."

"I'm just short," Vinita said, easing into a warm smile. "And my face is fat, which makes people look younger than they are—that's what they say, anyway."

"Twenty-eight?" Sammy said, narrowing his eyes a little.

"Do you want to see my God-damned passport?" Vinita snorted. She dug around in the front pocket of the black bag looped around her shoulder.

Sammy laughed. Gently grasped her hand out of the bag. "Would you like to get something to eat? Cinnamon buns?"

"Sure," Vinita said, relaxing her shoulders.

She was glad she didn't see Sammy's picture first, she decided, imagining he might have ended up in the NFC pile prematurely. He had taken a day off work (a successful software job with benefits) and flown from his new home in Texas (a small apartment with no washer and dryer, but he was new to the country, after all) to meet her in an airport. Nice enough, she thought.

He listened intently while she spoke. Ate his cinnamon bun with a knife and fork, wiping his moustache after each bite. Vinita ate hers with her fingers, licking icing from her fingertips before she flipped the *palloo* of her sari over her shoulder. She was not used to wearing a sari and the loose end fell off her shoulder each time she resumed eating. Her mother told her to safety-pin it to her bra, but she forgot the pin in her rush to leave. Sammy grabbed the material out of her coffee as she leaned forward for another bite.

"Shit," she said, looking immediately apologetic. The coffee bled through, leaving a dark rose-shaped stain in the butter yellow silk.

"Do you cook?" Sammy asked, passing her a stack of napkins.

"Cook?" she laughed.

"You appear to like food."

"What is that supposed to mean?"

She rubbed the stain. The napkin came apart in balls of paper and she finally gave up. "Yes, I love food. And you can't cook, I'm assuming, so I'd have to learn." She smiled at him, trying to picture his slender face without a moustache. "How hard can it be?"

They walked the main concourse of the airport, past kiosks that sold bitter coffee and cheap sunglasses. Sammy placed his hand on the small of her back in busy sections. They almost looked, Vinita thought, like a real couple on their way somewhere else.

At the security gate she smiled and kissed Sammy's cheek, not knowing *this* kiss and *this* smile had completed the negotiations. That by the time she reached Bombay and the waiting arms of aunties, she would be engaged. Her other appointments cancelled. Never meeting the boy on whose picture she wrote: *Kind, but homely.* The photograph she will tuck into her magazine, using him to keep her place in an article on skincare when her in-flight meal arrives. Forgetting him and her magazine on the plane.

Madeleine shouts from the shower, "Is that you, Will?"

"Who else would it be?"

"Read that piece of paper on the counter."

"What is it?" Will says, his voice trailing out the bathroom.

"Come back . . . it's a printout of my chat with Vinita," Madeleine hollers.

"Can't you just tell me what it says?"

"Read it." She can hear him exhale, settle against the bathroom vanity. "I think she should just leave him and go home—"

"Okay, let me read it already."

"Basically, she's a prisoner there." Madeleine sticks her hand out of the shower curtain, Will instinctively grabs the small bar of soap from beside the sink and places it in her palm.

"And soap," Will says, as though recording a mental shopping list. A habit that Madeleine finds slightly feminine but useful.

"She doesn't even drive. She has to cook all his meals."

"Am I reading or are you telling me the story?"

"I'm just upset."

"Don't you think you are being extreme? I mean, a *prisoner*..."

"How would you like being married to a stranger, living thousands of miles away from your family with no one to talk to?" She shuts off the water and throws back the curtain.

"I wouldn't. That's why I married you." His eyes fall momentarily to her breasts.

"Will ... please—" She grabs a towel off the hook on the back of the door and wraps it around herself. "You think it's that simple—she agreed to an arranged marriage, so therefore it's her fault."

"Pretty much. Look, I'm not saying I don't have sympathy. It's just, well, she chose it, didn't she?"

"Like she had a choice—please her family or please herself." Madeleine sits on the toilet lid, rubs her towel quickly up and down her legs.

"Doesn't sound like much of a choice."

"Yeah, for you. You hardly see your family. And you are all so horrifyingly polite." She walks past him into the dark bedroom. "Life isn't always polite. Polite doesn't always equal happy or content."

"You seem to have impolite and unhappy down to an art form."

Madeleine sighs. "It's just—I think I should help her."

Madeleine avoids Will's stare. Massages moisturizer into her warm face. She has been trying to come up with a solution to Vinita's unhappy situation. Last night she couldn't sleep, and as she watched the rise and fall of Will's chest she tried to imagine him a stranger. Imagined not knowing that he likes to sleep with his feet outside the covers, that he always picks the side of the bed closest to the window, that he falls asleep mid-sentence.

"You want her to come here?" Will says.

"No. I just think if she gets out of that environment she might have the courage to leave."

"That environment—you make it sound like—so she can't get a job, and he's quiet and sleeps a lot—am I missing something?"

"Apparently."

"I know she's an old friend, but telling her to leave her marriage. Is that something you want on your shoulders?" He pulls her toward him.

"I'm going to see how many Airmiles I have," she says into his neck. "Maybe I'll try to go home for a while and see if she'll come too."

"Stop calling it home. You *are* home."

"Let's not start with that again."

"Come on."

"I'm just worried about her." Madeleine pushes away and walks to the bedroom window, stares out at the white sky. She opens the window a crack and in the distance a train rumbles, its horn barely audible.

She and Vinita are now in daily contact. And Madeleine can no better explain her preoccupation with Vinita's situation to herself than to Will. She thinks of little else. Since the beginning of the week she has been sleeping poorly. Completing mundane household tasks once Will drifts off. Sewing buttons on the cuffs of Will's shirts last night, Madeleine thought of Vinita in Texas and wondered if she was up at the same time. Awoken by her husband's night jitters, the ones she told her about last week. *Myoclonic jerk*, Madeleine told her. The medical term for the problem. She'd looked it up on the Internet. Will has the same problem falling asleep, once elbowing Madeleine in the nose by mistake. She didn't wake him, though, and when the

tears came she was too exhausted to tell if she was crying from
resentment or pain.

"Why don't you call her?" Will says, tugging at Madeleine's
towel.

She sighs and turns towards him. "I think she wants it this
way." Her towel falls open and goosebumps spread across her
skin like a rash.

You there?

Madeleine heard the sound that accompanies Vinita entering the chatroom and ran to her study. It is 3:30. This is their
approved time. A half-hour window where Madeleine schedules no client meetings and Sammy is not yet home from
work.

What's going on?

I can't talk about it today. I'm too tired.
Okay?

Madeleine wants to reach for the phone. But she doesn't
want to lose the connection and so she follows Vinita's lead.

Okay. What are you cooking today?

I'm trying to make peas and rice.

You found pigeon peas in Texas?

No, silly. I brought cans with me. You should
have felt my suitcase.

And bird pepper? Did you bring any?

Are you crazy? They always check brown people
for shit like that. They expect us to travel with
live chickens.

Hell, Bahamians would.

You're telling me. Flying home once this woman
brought a damn frozen turkey on the plane.
Strapped the thing in the seat between us.

I have bird pepper.

Really! How much?

Two plastic bags full. I froze them. I bring them in my suitcase every time I'm home.

Jesus, mail some to me. They aren't going to check stuff coming from bloody Canada.

They'll smell it. A stinky envelope. Addressed to an Indian . . . you're the conspiracy theorist.

Maybe you could dry them in the oven first. Put them in at about 200.

Forget it. Just go to the store and buy chilies.

You know it's not the same.

Heat is heat, right?

Liar!

Madeleine laughs out loud. Thinks of the arguments she's had with Will each time he's brought home peppers as a peace offering after a fight. *I went grocery shopping. And no, that's not the amazing part . . . I found bird peppers.* She'd shake her head when he pulled them out of the plastic bag. She'd examine them, rubbing the pepper between her thumb and forefinger and tell him they were too big. That they looked Mexican.

It doesn't taste the same. I'll give you that, Madeleine types. The heat's harder to control.

Heat's always hard to control.

The thinner the hotter, as they say.

Now you talkin' nonsense girl, you know that's a lie. It's the colour of the skin.

Madeleine smiles at hearing the Vinita she misses.

The heat is in the placenta—the white ribs that run down the middle. Not in the pod colour.

Oh, Mrs. Pale Skin gets all smarty pants. Maybe you can figure out what's causing my rash? It tingles.

Stress. Lack of salt air. Now go back to your dinner and log in later to tell me how it tastes.

I should just make curry, you know. He's not

going to eat foreign food anyway. And the curry he likes is Indian, not Bahamian. Sammy says Caribbean curry is too simple. Those gypsy Indians away from home too long be forgetting how to cook.

When in doubt, add extra spice. Pepper masks anything.

Later, in her kitchen, Madeleine scours her shelf for *The Complete Book of Spices,* a colourful tome she received as a Christmas present from Will. Birds, she discovers, cannot taste the hotness in peppers. And the fruit of the bird pepper is so small that it is eaten whole by birds. Their gizzards break up the pods and the seeds pass through the animal undigested. But mammals, the book says, are discouraged by the extreme hotness of bird peppers. *In Texas, where they are called Turkey Peppers, wild birds intentionally eat a lot of them, which then flavors their flesh, making the turkeys distasteful to carnivores.*

"Smart turkeys," Madeleine says to herself. She pulls a baking sheet from the bottom drawer of the oven and a bag of peppers out of the freezer. There is frost forming on the inside of the bag, icicles covering some of the peppers. She throws the bag on the counter and flips to the section on drying.

Vinita pulls a chicken apart with her hands. Prising legs from sockets, separating fat from flesh. She pauses, as she must every few minutes, to wipe her greasy fingers on the dishcloth tucked into the waistband of her sari and dive a hand inside the folds of material to scratch the raised bumps that circle her waist. She resumes, trimming off wet curls of fat with a paring knife before throwing each piece of chicken into the hot oil of the pressure cooker. She has made this same dish—curried chicken—all twenty weeks she has lived in this apartment. *It's foolproof,* her mother told her and Vinita now agrees, thinking it is one of the few good pieces of advice she gave her. Sammy has complained about the sameness; has offered to call his mother in Calcutta for new recipes. Vinita refused, cooked a Bahamian meal one night. Peas and rice, baked macaroni and cheese, and fried fish. Sammy pushed the food around his plate, claiming foreign food didn't agree with his system. She now varies the vegetables in the chicken curry, adding eggplant and yellow pepper and even sweet potato to the shopping list. They go to the grocery store together on Saturdays and sometimes the mall. This is often Vinita's biggest outing of the week. Stores too far for her to walk. Their neighbourhood in a quiet corner of the city, an apartment building surrounded by the same houses in every direction, streets differentiated by the occasional fire hydrant or swing park.

She adds a handful of asparagus today and an extra spoonful of curry powder. The stems turn a satisfying emerald green. Sammy will be home for lunch soon. But she will not serve him this new dish. Lunchtimes, she heats up the leftovers from the night before. Setting them on the coffee table with a mug of sweet milky tea for 12:15 when he walks through the apartment door. The coffee table sits in the middle of the apartment, surrounded by worn pillows from the couch. The apartment came furnished, but missing a kitchen table, which the landlord promised to replace. Sammy tells Vinita he never missed the table when he lived alone. Mostly eating in front of the TV that sits directly in front of the coffee table on the carpet, the rabbit ears wrapped in tinfoil for better reception. She has complained, offered to call the landlord herself, but Sammy insists she doesn't. Says he'll handle it. He eats in silence, an *umhmm* or two as Vinita talks about her morning. That she watched an old episode of *One Day at a Time*. That she wonders why there were so many reruns on in the summer when more people are home from school or on vacation. She wipes her hands on the hem of her sari and flops on a pillow beside him. Steals chunks of chicken off his plate with her fingers.

"Why don't you get your own plate?"

"I'm not that hungry. You wouldn't be, either, if you had to mutilate a bloody carcass before cooking it?"

"Must you talk like that."

"Like what?"

Sammy naps after lunch. He carries his plate and fork to the kitchen counter and places them on an open magazine beside Vinita's cutting board. A gesture that, despite its helpful intent, irritates her as it forces her to stop her chopping and deal with the dish immediately. The counter space in the kitchen is limited and Vinita reserves this space for a magazine or book to flip through as she cooks. Sammy sleeps for the remainder of his lunch hour. Vinita wakes him at 12:50. Enough time for him to wash his face and change his shirt before returning to work.

"I have to go to the doctor," she says, plunking herself down on the bed beside him.

"Why?" Sammy rubs his eyes, looking more like a little boy than a thirty-three-year-old man.

"I think I'm allergic to something."

She lifts up her *salwar-kameez* and loosens the drawstring. Eyes the band of red dots on the left side of her torso and abdomen that thin out and disappear like the tail of a constellation on her right side.

"What? Something you ate?"

"No . . . I don't know. Maybe."

"It will probably just go away."

Vinita walks back to the kitchen. She shouts, "It's the damn expense, isn't it? Some of that wedding money is from my parents' friends."

She resumes cooking, mashes hot peppers and salt with a spoon on a wooden cutting board.

"I'm calling home tonight," she mumbles to herself.

Sammy walks to the front door, straightening his tie. He shakes his head. "It's too expensive."

She says nothing, grinds the fresh pepper into a bright orange stain.

Vinita had expected the banalities. Cooking and cleaning, snoring and burping. The almost comfortable silence where neither person feels the need to fill the void. Sitting beside each other but both alone in thought, the inches between them seemingly more like miles. But she had hoped she would adjust more easily to the melancholy drip of wet shirts hanging in the shower. The low ceiling of an apartment filled with old scents she could not distinguish but identified as the smell of failure. Burned meals, spilled drinks long dried and forgotten. Sometimes in the morning she stood in the bathroom and heard, echoing through the wall, the faint cry of other people's faucets, the squeak of feet on ceramic tubs.

At first Sammy had seemed serious and quiet, but also easygoing—the exact opposite of her. She launched herself into her life, reading the notes on cooking she had scrawled on a notepad as her mother gave her a quick lesson before she left Nassau, wearing her saris and s*alwar-kameez* daily, relishing the time a uniform afforded her. She wore a *bindi* sticker. Touching it incessantly at first, finally letting it be when she lost one in a pot of curry. She wore her hair in a practical ponytail and occasionally lined her eyes with *kohl*. In this new place she would be transformed into a different woman. Here she would be as domestic as a stained wooden cutting board, faintly smelling of onions.

Madeleine's suitcase reeks of pepper. The freezer bags she brings each time she returns from Nassau. Pepper she cannot get in Calgary, not even at the West Indian grocery. "Pepper smuggler," Will laughs. Telling her she's on her own with Customs Canada each time she checks *No* next to *Are you carrying food or plant material?* At home she keeps the pepper in the freezer, uses it for special occasions. To season fish or curry or baked macaroni and cheese. She crushes the pepper on a small dish, careful to wash her hands before touching her eyes or mouth. She measures it out jealously for dinner guests, telling Will that most Canadians can't take the heat. That she's not wasting it on people who will wash it away with milk and bread as soon as it hits their tongues. "That *is* spicy," they'll say, Madeleine smiling at Will and passing the breadbasket.

Will sweats when he eats spicy food. But never complains. He asks, "Is this towel worthy?" when he sees her mashing pepper on the cutting board. Water pours from his head, soaking the collar of his shirt. Madeleine sometimes adds an extra pepper to see if he notices. He just smiles and says, "You won't kill me that easily."

"What are you doing?" Will says as he walks into the living room where Madeleine has dragged two suitcases out of the hallway closet.

"I just thought I'd get stuff together in case I have to go."

"Go?"

"For Vinita."

"I thought we discussed this."

"So did I. And you said you understood." Madeleine holds the suitcase open. "Does this smell like pepper?"

"All our luggage smells like pepper," Will says, still standing.

And it is true. Madeleine hadn't noticed it until today. The musty food odour that seemed to have leached into the walls and carpet of the storage closet. It smelled like a foreign country. All those things that were impossible to get at home. She figured Will had smelled it this way all along. But he couldn't appreciate the way it made her feel.

"It's like my Abuela's cutting board," Madeleine says quietly, pressing her hand into her nose, inhaling deeply.

"I can imagine," Will says.

"Can you?" Madeleine says.

Will steps over the suitcase and sits on the couch behind her. "So, have you and Vinita made plans, then?"

"There's no plan, Will. That's what you think? That I just sit here scheming, looking for trouble? Is that what you think?"

"I don't know what you think about, to tell you the truth."

"Like it's some big mystery."

"Maybe we are thinking about the same thing."

"What's that?" she says, looking over her shoulder.

He lies back on the couch, pulls a pillow to his chest and rests his chin on it. He drums his thick fingers on the cushion in the manner he does when he is thinking of the next thing to say.

"Say it," Madeleine says, shutting the suitcase with a gratifying *click click*. "I know what you are thinking. That I'm getting too involved. That this is the kind of intensity I only give to other people's lives." And she knows it's true. She idly rubs her hand over the top of the suitcase and says, "Do you know why people get married?"

"Why?"

"Distraction."

"Here I thought people did it to feel loved and supported and even happy."

"Happy?" Madeleine pulls the suitcases into the hallway, lifting them just enough to not scratch the wooden floor.

"We could use the points to buy new luggage, I guess," Madeleine says, testing the waters.

"So it can get stunk up too?"

"Maybe I shouldn't—"

"What?"

"Nothing."

"Go on. What?"

"Forget it."

"Use the stupid points," Will says, curling up onto the couch and closing his eyes.

"For the suitcases?" She bites her bottom lip.

"For whatever." He yawns and rolls towards the back cushions. His face no longer visible. "Madeleine, I'm not stopping you from doing anything."

Madeleine receives a package from Vinita in the mail. Five and a half metres of turquoise silk. She thinks it's curtains at first, the most beautiful she has ever seen. She rips it out of its brown paper and holds it up to the window—eyeing the green couch she's wanted to get rid of since she and Will married two years ago. A shade that is difficult to match with anything. The turquoise cloth sits draped across a black curtain rod until she contacts Vinita and discovers it's a sari.

I always thought they came in two pieces.

No, silly. Shit, I forgot to include a cholee and a petticoat. Just wear a tank top and a long slip.

How do I do it? Madeleine types, fabric wrapped around her like a shawl.

Start with the waist. Tuck the plain end into your underwear all the way around. Right to left. Make sure that the end touches the floor.

Madeleine stands up from the computer, tucks and loops the fabric around her body as per Vinita's instructions.

Bring it up under your right arm and over your left shoulder so it falls to about your knees.

By the time she finishes, Madeleine looks like a poorly wrapped mummy. She had expected to look exotic. The soft silk against her skin, trailing behind her.

God, you'd laugh if you saw me.

I wish I could.

Madeleine settles back in the office chair.

I wish I could see you too.

She unwraps herself when Vinita signs off, and she looks on the Internet for instructions. Finds a suitable site with step-by-step directions. *Start making pleats in the sari, about 5 inches deep. . . . Make about 7 to 10 pleats and hold them up together so that they fall straight and even. . . . Tuck the pleats into the waist slightly to the left of the navel. . . . Drape the remaining fabric around yourself once more. . . . The end portion thus* draped is the palloo, and can be prevented from slipping off by fixing it at the shoulder to the blouse with a small safety pin.

There are diagrams of a perfect woman draping the cloth around her effortlessly. And further down, a story:

Once upon a time, a King held a grand and glorious bow-and-arrow competition. Princes from all over India took part, including the five Pandava brothers and the one hundred Kurava brothers. The prize was the King's beautiful daughter Draupadi's hand in marriage. It was a hard competition. The winner had to have skill and courage. The competition was close, but on the last shot one of the Pandava brothers won. Victorious, they took Draupadi home and all five brothers lived happily with her as their wife.

Months later, the Kurava brothers had a dice-throwing competition. The Pandava brothers were invited to their kingdom to play. Draupadi went with them. The excitement of the competition built so that everybody was betting all he owned to win. One of the Pandava brothers became carried away with the game and said, "The winners of the game may take home the beautiful Draupadi."

The game went for days and days. In the end the Pandava brothers lost. They gave Draupadi to the Kurava brothers and then left the kingdom for home with very sad hearts.

The Kurava brothers were very cruel and wanted to have fun with their new prize. So they ordered their guards to drag Draupadi by her lovely hair to the farthest hall in the palace and to strip her of all her clothes.

The guards did what they were told. They caught one end of the diaphanous material that draped Draupadi so demurely, yet seductively, and began to unwrap her. They kept pulling and pulling and pulling. And the cloth kept coming. After trying for some time, all the guards had was a huge mound of cloth with Draupadi, still fully covered, in the middle of her sari.

Unknown to the guards, the invisible god Krishna was watching. And had used his power to make her sari endless.

The news of the Kurava brothers' antics eventually reached their father. He quickly stormed into the hall where the guards were still trying to undress Draupadi and ordered them to stop. He scolded his sons and had Draupadi returned to her real husbands, the Pandava brothers, where she lived until the end of her days.

Madeleine pictures Vinita in the endless sari. The beautiful prize at the centre. And wonders if she hadn't been wrong in rejecting Vinita's assertion that a love marriage and an arranged marriage only differed in who did the arranging.

Madeleine wears the sari for the rest of the day. Fingering the elegant silk while on the phone, catching it under her feet while walking, trailing the material into her food as it falls off her shoulder. It turns out that wearing a sari is a skill in and of itself. She catches a glimpse of herself and the wrinkled sari in the mirror and takes it off. Spreads the cloth across the ironing board, the end pooling on the floor. She presses it, little by little, adjusting the heat when the colour starts to deepen, until the delicate silk is smooth and polished. Once she is done she is reluctant to put it on again. To ruin its clean lines. She folds it along with a sandalwood sachet and puts it in her bottom drawer, like a secret, with bikinis and sarongs she only wears on vacation.

Sammy brings treats home from the cafeteria at work. Food that would otherwise be thrown out at the end of the day. A bagel with a serving-size container of cream cheese, the garnish wilting. A sticky Danish with Saran wrap imbedded in the lemon-yellow centre. A piece of cake, dry at the edges with icing stuck to the top of the plastic. Vinita sits cross-legged on the carpet in front of the coffee table, spreading the plastic boxes like a banquet. She loves the Danish. Licks the plastic wrap greedily, savouring the moment. She watches Indian movies while she eats, catching only some of the words. Fixated on the women thrusting their hips in unison. Sammy's family sends the videos in the big brown envelopes that arrive each month from India. She wanted to open the first package when it arrived, hoped it was a wedding present. It was addressed to Sammy, but as his wife—the cooker of his meals and the doer of his laundry—she thought it acceptable to open his mail. She ripped the corner of the package, then stopped. The envelope was lined with bubble wrap, she could only make out a videocassette and a tiny glass bottle—another ingredient she would no doubt have to look up on the Internet or e-mail her mother about. She tried to reseal the envelope. Licking the stale glue, pressing her sweaty finger into the brown paper. When Sammy arrived home, he eyed the package expectantly, carrying it through to the bedroom when he went to change his clothes. He said nothing about the tear when he reappeared with a video and magazine, which he placed on the coffee table, saying, "These are especially for you, from my mother."

When the latest package arrives, she can hear the ripping of paper and the rustle of bubble wrap from the living room. "Anything interesting?" she shouts, only half expecting an answer.

"Yes."

"What then?" She spreads the cream cheese on the bagel.

"Just hellos."

"Like what?" She rolls her eyes.

Vinita has come to love the packages as much as Sammy. Package days are his most talkative. She can expect more than the usual silence from his end of the coffee table. Complimenting her cooking, asking if she might like to go to the mall on the weekend to look for drapes to replace the bedsheets he has used as window covering since he moved into his apartment last year. She has even accepted the ritual surrounding the mail. The way he insists on leaving the parcel unopened until after supper when he places his plate on the kitchen counter and goes to the bedroom to open it alone. She once knocked on the door but he wouldn't let her in, insisted he'd be out in a moment, that he liked to open the packages himself. There was a childlike quality to his voice and Vinita found herself unwilling to question him further.

He walks out of the bedroom, holding a small green container. "Maybe we could try this on your rash?"

"What is it?"

"Salve from my mother."

"God, I really must be allergic to something," she says, lifting her tunic. "It's getting worse." She rubs a tentative hand over her belly where the spots have become blisters filled with fluid.

"What do you think it is?"

"I think it's you."

He says nothing.

"Get it? Maybe I'm allergic to you." Vinita straightens her clothes, eats another bite of cake. "God, sometimes I wonder about you—it's called a sense of humour."

She sits at the foot of the bed on a pillow as Sammy rubs the salve into her shoulders where the rash has now spread. The oily mixture smells of sandalwood and melts against her hot skin.

"I should still go to the doctor."

"See if this works first."

He falls asleep before her. She reads a magazine, scraping the pages on the top of the sheet as she turns them. Sammy's arms jerk and he looks momentarily like a puppet, arms suspended by guide wires. Vinita gives a snort of satisfaction, imagining each flinch an interrupted dream. Sammy claims dreams are indulgences and that his sleep is dreamless. She sets down the magazine and watches him. This quiet man she married, who changes for bed in the bathroom and leaves his pajama top on when they make love. But she is happy for this. Glad that he is gentle and fast, that he doesn't look her in the eye when he is inside her. That when she steals a look at him, he looks as single-minded as when

he does crossword puzzles in bed. It is over when his penis, warm
and soft like a bloated piece of pasta, slips out unexpectedly. Sliding between her legs on to the dry bedsheet.

Madeleine has cookbooks stacked beside the bed. Menus running through her head. Fried Jacks. Mutton souse. She has baking sheets filled with bird peppers spread across the kitchen.
Lined with wax paper the way her mother suggested when she
called her long distance for instructions. The smell permeates
every inch of the house. Squeezes through the small gap in the
window so Will could smell them as he walked up to the front
door earlier this evening.

"It smells like BO in here," he said, retreating to the bedroom. He appeared half an hour later, hungry. Announced he
was going out for pizza if Madeleine wanted to join him. She
didn't.

All afternoon, Madeleine has inspected the peppers. Cut the
tops off with her sharpest knife. Saving as much of the tiny fruit
as she could. She lined thirty on the first pan, then started on
the second. She filled the oven and looked around for spaces to
lay other pans. The kitchen counters covered, she placed the
last two on the coffee table. All these years of gingerly doling
out peppers. Now she feels deprived. Like she has somehow
depleted a store of energy. Or weakened a muscle. One that
quickly atrophies without use.

She stopped working when all the peppers were set in neat
rows, drying quickly, she hoped, in the parched prairie air.
Madeleine washed her hands in almost scorching water before
going to bed. Using a brush on her fingernails. Her cuticles
burning. But she knew she couldn't clean all of it off. She had
read somewhere that even repeated hand washing with hot
water and soap cannot fully remove the capsicum oils. That she
should avoid touching any mucous membrane until her hands
were free of the poison.

She brought the cookbooks to bed. Started looking for recipes to test the dried peppers before she mailed them to Vinita. Madeleine and Will haven't spoken since he came back from supper. She didn't hear him when he came in. She was crouched in front of the oven door, looking to see if she could see any signs of progress in the trays that had the benefit of the oven lamp. He walked by in silence. Annoyed, Madeleine supposed, that she chose the peppers over him.

Now in bed, Madeleine puts the cookbook down and says, "I was thinking, we had a sort of arranged marriage?"

"What are you talking about?"

"My mother."

"What?"

"She liked you so much. You know, when we were just friends. She was always saying, *Madeleine, you should just—*"

"Your mother liked me. And that makes our marriage arranged?"

"It's not as simple as that."

"Okay, I have to confess something—you know that goat in my parents' backyard? Your parents gave it to them as a dowry."

"Listen to me."

"I'm listening, Maddie, you're just not making any sense."

"I'm just saying sometimes women arrange their own marriages to transform themselves into someone else. Someone less passionate, less dangerous."

"Dangerous? Are you threatening me?"

"Jesus."

"What's with you?"

1 large onion. 4 chilies. 5 potatoes. Madeleine resumes reading her book.

"I'm making roti tomorrow for supper," she says.

"Madeleine, you don't have to cook for me."

"I'll make some chicken roti and some vegetable." She continues reading.

What are you thinking? Madeleine types.

That I haven't worn my jeans for six months. I
don't think they still fit me.

Go buy new ones.

Too expensive. Sammy's right . . . without me
working.

Forget Sammy. . . . How's the rash?

Bad. Full of pus.

Did you think about what I said?

Maybe I just need to be patient.

It's okay to admit you made a mistake.

Jesus, stop pushing.

Sorry.

Maybe this is just the way it is. You're not
that happy.

Happier than you.

Like that's saying something. Maybe it's just
like this.

Come on.

Madeleine stops typing. Straightens from her hunched position. She takes a sip from the cold coffee sitting next to her keyboard. What does she want? She wants to ask Vinita if she feels it too, time slipping away from them. She wants to ask if she remembers how they used to talk about Madeleine moving back to Nassau after university. That they'd live side by side in townhouses in Cable Beach. She's sure she can hear the longing behind Vinita's simple words. Madeleine thinks of their summer together in Nassau and feels the distance like a hole in her chest. She writes, When's the last time you remember being happy?

What do you mean?

Remember that summer? Madeleine stops, unsure whether to continue.

Vinita writes, When you were home?

Yeah.

Remember that guy from the gas station?

How could I forget? I was the one baking in the hot car while you two—

God, I haven't thought about him in years.

Madeleine rubs her finger over the rim of her coffee cup. Looks at her hands, dry from scrubbing the pepper out from under her nails.

I think about that summer all the time.

Madeleine sets her chin in her hands. Remembers the day she left the car and walked around the back of the house Vinita and the boy were in. Crept behind the pear tree in her blouse and skirt. High heels sinking into the earth. She looked through the louvred glass window and saw nothing but a small room with a large bookcase and a reading chair. As she walked back around to the front, she heard a voice over her shoulder.

"Lookin' for something spicy?" the man sitting on the stone wall asked, his eyes travelling down Madeleine's body. He was eating a hot meat patty, dipping it into some sauce in a plastic container. He was wearing jeans. His T-shirt tied around his head. Sweat soaking through the material in a dark halo.

Madeleine looked up, momentarily frozen in place. She took a deep breath. Thought about calling to Vinita, then hesitated, wondering how to explain what she was doing in the backyard.

"*Dis* too peppery for you, Goldilocks," said the man, hopping down on the other side of the wall. Madeleine ran her hand through her sun-bleached hair as she hurried back to the car.

Back in the kitchen, Madeleine can't stop thinking about what to make with the dried bird peppers. And how much longer they will keep in this new form. Has she solved anything by drying them? Or just wasted the supply that was to last her until next Christmas's visit? She presses a thumb into one of the peppers, which crumbles easily. And thinks about everything she will tell Vinita when she sees her.

Will comes home earlier than usual. Madeleine is still in her study when she hears the sound of his shoes dropping at the front door. When she hears him approach, she starts typing. "Come in," she shouts when he knocks at the door. "I wasn't expecting you so early."

"Don't let me stop you."

Will puts his hands on Madeleine's shoulders. She lets his cold hands sit there for a moment, then shrugs him off. The keywords she has typed into the search engine read: *rash + poisoning*.

"Sounds cheery," Will says, moving towards the door.

Madeleine ignores him. "There's curry on the stove." She starts to type again.

"How's she doing?"

"Not good."

"I'm sorry to hear that."

"I'll be down in a bit," she says. "The food will get cold."

"I'm not hungry."

"I spent an hour and a half cooking."

"Did something new happen?"

"There's *naan* bread in the oven, Vinita e-mailed me the recipe."

Madeleine scrolls down the screen, choosing among the list of hits she received.

"What are you looking for?" Will says, tilting his head to look at the monitor.

"I think I found it."

"What?"

"What's causing Vinita's rash." She doesn't look up. "Shit, no."

"You know what I think—"

"Please just go and eat supper."

Will touches Madeleine's shoulder. She shrugs his hand off. He opens his mouth to say something. Turns around instead and walks towards the door.

Madeleine watches him walk away. She drinks her cup of

coffee. Watches the light outside her window begin to fade, and her stomach grumbles. Soon she will have to turn on the lights. But there is still a little time, so she scrolls through the lists and lists of possibilities, looking for the right one. She can hear the beep of the microwave downstairs. And the clank of Will digging through the dishwasher for a fork.

"It's good," he shouts up the stairs.

"Too hot?"

"No."

But Madeleine can hear his sharp intake of breath, even from her study.

Vinita stopped eating bread last week. And sugar and dairy. She thinks her inflammation might be food-induced. She still prepares Sammy's regular meals, licking her fingers greedily as she works, hoping traces of sugar or wheat don't cause another flare-up. She makes herself a simple salad with the five-dollar bottle of tamari dressing that Sammy reluctantly bought for her at the health food store. Tonight she made Sammy *gulabjamun* for dessert. He picks at it. She clears the dishes, pressing her finger into the syrupy sauce, sucking on it as she rinses the plate.

"Maybe she's right." Vinita says. "It could be stress."

"I beg your pardon?" Sammy says, walking to his room to change.

"The rash. Never mind, you'll just say I am overreacting." Her voice trails off.

"I will send for more cream."

"No. I don't want more of that green shit all over me."

Vinita pours herself a drink. A bottle of rum at the back of the cupboard she imagines was there when Sammy moved in. The level has not changed since she arrived and the cap is difficult to remove. Sticky with traces down the side of the glass. She doesn't mix it, drinks it straight from a red plastic cup she uses to water the plants. She turns the handle on the bedroom door. She has rehearsed this for weeks. The way she will hold her mouth, her hands. What she will be wearing. That she will be packed already. He sits on the edge of the bed in white briefs and grey socks, rubbing his hands over and over his face, in a motion that seems to Vinita more comforting than anxious. *Don't use his name. Not even if you are pushed, don't use his name.* She clears her throat.

"I'm leaving," she says, tightening her hand around the glass.

"I know," Sammy says.

"You know." She narrows her eyes, takes another sip from the cup. She can feel her heart beating in her head.

"That's all you have to say?" She shakes her head in disbelief. "Would have been nice if you had tried to stop me."

"When are you going?"

She hears in his voice an unfamiliar insistence.

"I don't know." She walks out of the room.

"Don't do this—" He follows her into the living room.

"Or what? What are you going to do to me?"

"Don't be like this."

She downs the remainder of her drink, thicker and sweeter at the bottom of the glass. Her lips curl into an involuntary sneer.

"This serves me right, I suppose."

"What is so wrong?"

"Wrong!" she shouts, pulling her coat off the hook beside the front door. "I have been living with you for five months and I have no idea who the hell you are. There's something missing."

"What?" he shouts, raising his voice for the first time Vinita can remember. "You think I'm lacking something, some quality you are looking for in a husband? Maybe it's you."

"Excuse me?"

"You are selfish," he says, hesitating. "A selfish bitch."

She slaps him. An almost unconscious act like tucking a piece of loose hair behind her ear, or flipping her *palloo* over her shoulder as she does dozens of times a day. She stands motion-less at the door and looks at him. Harmless in his white under-wear and socks, his belly a small, hairy ball of flesh. She considers for a moment the fact that this is the most naked she has ever seen him in daylight. His legs as wiry and pale as she had expected. She rubs her palm with her fingers and thinks if it weren't for the tingle in her fingers she could almost believe it never happened. That she had thought of slapping him, but couldn't follow through. She feels strangely disembodied and thinks of the time her mother caught her in the back of the house with a boy from school. *This is going to hurt me more than it will hurt you.* He steps towards her and stops. "You are too selfish to be anyone's wife," he says. Slumps against the wall, his soft arms at his side.

Will comes home from work to find Madeleine sitting in her sari at the kitchen table. She is painting her toenails, crossing her legs so she can dangle one foot and admire the purple jewel shade she sweeps onto her big toe. Every inch of the kitchen is spotless. Gone are the trays of peppers that blanketed the coun-tertops. The coffee maker and pasta jars back in their usual place. The air is heavy with the acetone mixed with Pine Sol. On top of the stove where the baking trays have been sitting for days is a large stockpot. The lid clanking occasionally as the contents bubble.

"Do you think I have pretty toes?" Madeleine asks, turning to look at Will.

"What's with the getup?"

"Don't you think I look nice?"

"Is everything okay?"

"Fine," she says. She sits up and adjusts the waistband of the sari.

"What's all this about?"

"I finally found the perfect recipe for the peppers," Madeleine says, pushing herself out of the chair. She breezes past him to the stove, flipping the sari over her shoulder with a flourish. She slips her sandals on, careful not to smudge her polish.

"Okayyy," Will says. Holding his face in a neutral expression. "I'm just going to change." He motions up the stairs.

"Yeah, go ahead." She lifts the lid on the pot and stirs the thick chowder. "Hurry up. I'm starved."

Madeleine closes the pot and looks at her reflection in the lid. Rubs away crimson lipstick that clings to the corners of her mouth.

Will shouts down the stairs, "You didn't use *all* the peppers in that, did you?"

"It says in one of my cookbooks that Bahamian bird peppers are one of the hottest in the world."

Will comes into the kitchen and sits on a stool beside the stove. "Madeleine, I can't begin to understand what is going on with you and Vinita's situation. I just want you to know if you have to—"

Madeleine puts her fingers up to Will's lips. "You're going to love this," she says, lifting the lid to scoop the thick soup into a bowl. She sets it in front of Will on the counter.

"I got a call from her today," Madeleine says.

"That's great. What did she say?"

"She's back home." Madeleine digs through the cutlery drawer.

"So she left him?"

"Did you know the chicken-pox virus can lie dormant in your body for years?" Madeleine says, placing a spoon next to the bowl.

"What are you talking about?"

"Shingles. That's what she has."

"So she's going back?"

"I don't know," she says, motioning to the food. "They put pepper on it."

"On what?"

"The shingles. Capsaicin cream. It's the chemical that gives pepper heat."

"Jesus. They put that on a rash?"

"Pepper deadens the nerve endings." She pushes the food in front of him. "It numbs the painful areas."

Madeleine takes a deep breath. For weeks she has been imagining what Vinita's life was like in Texas. But what can anyone know about someone else's life? She looks at Will and a memory overtakes her. Will on their wedding day. The middle of one of the hottest summers in Nassau. Madeleine picked the cathedral with no air conditioning. The priest's sweat ran in a rivulet off his chin and into the open Bible as they exchanged vows. Will's shirt collar transparent by the end of the one-hour ceremony.

Will leans down and takes a long whiff of the bowl, then looks at Madeleine.

"What?" Madeleine says. "Go ahead and try it."

Will takes a scoop and puts it into his mouth. Madeleine watches the rosiness spread across his cheeks. She knows he will eat every last drop, never complaining that it's too hot. He leans over the bowl, elbow out as he spoons it into his mouth. A faraway look crosses his face. An expression Madeleine finds difficult to read. Thinking for a moment how strange it is that resignation is harder to detect than anger.

PICTURE THIS

WE ARRIVE THE DAY BEFORE THE VIEWING. MY FAMILY POSTPONES IT so we can see my grandmother's body before friends and neighbours. The body is prepared as we sit in airports—Dallas, Miami—trying to read magazines, running through the checklist of items my mother has asked us to buy. Dong qui, oil of oregano, arnica, angelica. Herbs my mother says she can't get on the island. We had no time once we received the call. Oldest Auntie speaking calmly into my ear, "Sweetheart, get home—immediately." She said it as if it were a place just around the corner. As though it didn't take fourteen hours and three airplanes to get home.

The airplane doors open and everything is in slow motion. The heavy smell of salt air laced with fuel, the slow, rising scream of cicadas in the bushes that line the runways, and the weight of my heels that press heavy into the warmed asphalt. I stop a moment to adjust my carry-on, sweat forming under the strap, and tug my damp blouse from my chest. My husband squeezes my shoulder as we walk past the baggage carousel and out the swinging doors through which we can see Small Auntie waving towards us in the crowd.

By the time her car pulls onto JFK Drive, Small Auntie is making lists. Her habit in situations she can't fully control. "Pallbearer, proofreader, airport pick-up. . . ." She assigns us duties. "Drop luggage, egg salad sandwiches, florist's tape, bags of ice. . . ." Small Auntie digs in her purse as she drives, passes each of us small gold crucifixes. "Stockings, film, death certificate. . . ." She interrupts her inventory to correct my husband, who is pinning on the cross, "No, the right side. Like this." He glances at me in the back seat with the fear and bewilderment of a POW. "The Smiths, the Hannas, the Rolles, the Careys, the hat lady. . . ." I rest my head on a suitcase and flop my arm over my other ear. I look out the window at the telephone poles and palm trees that line the road like soldiers leading us to the body.

The funeral home parking lot is full. My family drove here in a convoy. It's how they travel. To dinner, to church. "Are you all leaving now?"—the call placed between houses so everyone ends up on West Bay Street at the same time, heading in the same direction. Small Auntie says they have been here since the funeral home opened this morning. That they've been leaving in shifts to eat. That they made the funeral director move the body to a different *slumber* room. One closer to the entrance, with a better view of the garden and easier access for tomorrow's visitors.

The sun is setting as we step into the courtyard. The marble walkway is lined with a respectful row of yellow and red crotons. My husband walks inside the slumber room, but I stop outside the large wooden doors and look at *her* name slipped into the slot on the wall. "I don't think I can do this," I say to no one in particular, "I don't need to see her."

"Come," Small Auntie grabs me by the elbow. "You have to

say goodbye. She looks beautiful." Small Auntie pushes the heavy door with her free arm and motions to someone inside. My mother and Oldest Auntie appear out of the darkness of the room. Soft music is playing and I can hear the din of my family reciting the rosary. A hand pulls me inside and I stand at the back of the small room, waiting for my pupils to adjust. Chairs in a horseshoe around the coffin. Mahogany with brass handles, it sits on a pedestal in front of a crucifix and a wall of white curtains. Pretty Cousin standing at the foot of the coffin with a camera. *Click, click.* A picture of everyone in the chairs. Then Pretty Cousin leans over the coffin and kisses our grandmother on the lips. "There's an eyelash trapped under her makeup," she says, leaning in further, "should I take it off?" She is hunched over the body now, inspecting the skin with her fingernail. *Click, click.*

I look around the room for some kind of reaction. No one says a thing. They have been with the body for a day now. Slept in chairs outside the morgue until morning when she was safely transferred to the funeral home. Promised in whispers and squeezing of hands that they would not leave her alone until it was done. Until she was securely in the ground. Diplomat Auntie walks toward me. "Come, child, it's almost time to leave," she says. "Come see her."

I move in front of the body and turn my head so no one can see my tears. I hear the funeral director at the door with a reminder about closing time. I breathe in and move my hand as if to touch her, then hold back. I hold my breath.

"I don't want to be here," I say and purse my lips tightly. Behind me is the clamour of everyone gathering to leave, discussing tomorrow's plan. Deciding who will stay in the parking lot tonight.

The shadow of a coconut tree flickers behind the curtain. And I remember the fragile light in her bedroom the last morning I saw her alive. Early morning before I left for the airport to go back to Canada.

When I turn around they have all left the room. I can hear them on the other side. I stand in front of the coffin and look at her wrinkles filled with stage makeup—the consistency of syrup. My eyes pan down her body to her hands, which are clasped on her chest, a rosary entwined in her cold fingers.

The baby's not sick, but we feed her medicine before the funeral. It's Oldest Auntie's idea. "She'll cry through the funeral if we don't," she says, looking at the baby wriggling in my arms. "Won't you?" Oldest Auntie presses out her lips in a pucker. Her mouth a polished mocha colour, lips perfectly lined like every other woman's in my family. The kind of lipstick that leaves waxy rings on wineglasses and burgundy smudges on cheeks. I swing the baby away from her and look out the kitchen door into the living room. The rest of my family mills about, dressed in black, while the air conditioner whines in protest. They stand adjusting Windsor knots and hatpins in the mirror. Pretty Cousin is taking pictures. *Say sexy. Smile.*

"Maybe we should wait?" I say.

"For what?"

"She might fall asleep on her own."

"We can't take the chance," Oldest Auntie says. "Give her to me."

I step away. Pretty Cousin moves toward us with the camera. *Say Sexy, baby. Sexy baby.* I shake my head and duck into the kitchen before the shutter opens.

"It's grape cough medicine, for God's sake. It tastes good." Oldest Auntie grins at the baby, kisses her little mouth. I turn the baby away from my body, hold her out like a package. "Hold still. Say ahh." Oldest Auntie parts her lips. "Like this, child. Make the noise the birdies make. *Ooh, hoo, ooh, hoo.*" The baby laughs at the dove sound and sticks out her pink tongue.

I set her down on the kitchen counter and wipe a trickle of

purple syrup off her bottom lip with my thumb. I lick my finger clean. "All gone," I say, looking down at her round face. "All gone."

"Now do something with her hair," Oldest Auntie says, walking out of the kitchen. "The limousines will be here in ten minutes."

I run my hand through the baby's mass of curls. Pull the hair off her face and pin it in place with a clip from my own hair. She looks perfect in her navy blue dress. Her mother—Pretty Cousin—decided she was too young for black. The dress has a white collar and three embroidered ducks across the chest. The baby has ruby earrings and a matching gold bracelet with a tiny stone embedded in the centre. I carry her into the living room and look at us together in the mirror. Framed by the gilded gold. "Picture perfect," I say, kissing the top of her head.

Later I will hold the sleeping baby in front of me like a shield as I walk down the aisle of the dim church toward the daylight. This is the picture I will remember. Her protecting me from sympathetic hands and faces. A woman tracing a worrying finger down the curve of the baby's spine.

I can't tell which one is my mother. She and her sisters are all wearing black mantillas and from behind they look identical. Mournful brides, black lace pooling on their shoulders. I recognize my mother as she turns her head to look as the coffin is pulled from the hearse. I know it is her, the way she watches the pallbearers' feet as they move into the graveyard. Counting steps.

"We decided the granddaughters shouldn't wear veils," my mother says this morning, ironing mantillas in high heels and a black satin slip. "We think you girls should wear hats." *We* is her and her four sisters. Oldest Auntie, Diplomat Auntie, Small Auntie and Tall Auntie. Any combination or permutation. Sometimes it only takes two of them to decide something. A huddle in the doorway, a conversation in the bathroom—one of them plucking her eyebrows, the other on the toilet. When *it* is decided you hear heels clicking down the hall in unison. That certain look once their minds are made up. Like something swallowed whole. "*We* think hats are best," my mother says as she grabs a bottle of spray starch from the end of the ironing board. Points it at the door like a pistol. Then back at the ironing board. "Go see the hats," she says behind the cloud of starch.

There's a cupboard at the end of the hall, carefully stacked with hatboxes. Diplomat Auntie started keeping them there when she ran out of space on her bedroom floor. *Bumper Brim, Capeline, Mushroom, Sailor, Wedding Ring.* Each name listed on the lid of a different hatbox. The hats stuffed with tissue paper to support the crowns. Diplomat Auntie comes out of her room where she is dressing to assign appropriate head covering. "Your face is too big for the brim," she tells Pretty Cousin. "Try this." Between hats the constant *click, click* of the camera. The sound makes me smile out of reflex before I turn my head away from the lens. "Sexy," echoes the baby crawling about our legs.

Diplomat Auntie picks a wide-brimmed Bandino for me. "Your face can support it," she says. I don't argue. I point out a knuckle-sized divot in the front of the crown. "Easy fix, sweetheart," she says, carrying it into the kitchen. Diplomat Auntie boils the kettle on the stove. I pass her the hat and she positions the dent over the jet of steam. She pushes out the dent with practised fingers. "Blow on it here." She points to the repaired patch. I blow gently and the material stiffens. I put the hat on and look in the mirror.

"Say cheese." I lean down to grab the camera away, bump Pretty Cousin in the head with the lip of my hat. "It's like a force field," she says. "No one can get near you."

She holds up the camera. "Come on. Just you by yourself." I step out of frame. The only sign of me is the brim of my hat—a blur in the upper-right corner of the shot.

I don't notice the flowers in the church until an altar boy knocks over a vase. The house is packed with the same bouquets. Two days before the funeral Diplomat Auntie announced, "We have run out of space." The new arrivals replaced day-olds, which were moved to the Bahama room to wilt in the heat. My father moved the TV off some antique trunks and pushed them against the wall in the living room. Diplomat Auntie cleared the sideboard of porcelain figurines and stored them in the utility room. Moved a lamp off a mahogany table onto the tiled floor. Scanned the house for surfaces, forgotten side tables, ottomans.

Click, click. A cascade of white lilies hits the marble floor in the church. The altar boy surprised by the flash. Pretty Cousin holding her camera against her stomach for a stealth snap. She miscalculates the angle. Points the camera toward the floor. A picture of nothing. A picture of the spot where the flowers *will* land.

There must be three dozen in this vase alone. When the altar boy bends down to gather the flowers, the Monsignor motions to him to stop picking them up. My mother is in front of me and whispers something to Small Auntie. I am afraid she will excuse herself from the pew and start cleaning up flowers in the middle of the service. I tuck my chin to my chest and pray she doesn't ask me to pick them up.

"*Las flores,*" she'll whisper in Spanish, the way she and her sisters do when wanting to convey something delicate or offensive in public. "*Las flores.*" And with this simple declaration I suspect she means, "Clean them up, it would be shameful for one of us not to do it."

I lift my eyes and see my mother handing Tall Auntie a handkerchief. I feel momentarily guilty for assuming the worst. And then I hear her say it, "*Las flores.*" With one nod of her head Tall Auntie has the altar boy on his knees, cradling wet lilies in his arms. Details are her job. Tall Auntie had her interior designer decorate the church. "Do it up right," were her only instructions.

The altar is filled from floor to ceiling with white flowers. Roses, lilies, freesia and frangipani perfume the heavy air. I catch a whiff as a wall fan oscillates across my face. Among the flowers sits one large potted palm tree. A royal palm strategically placed in front of the side door Diplomat Auntie's protocol officer said would disrupt flow if left open—stopping a careless guest from entering through the side as a VIP walks from the back.

There is a seating plan. Small Auntie typed it on the computer last night. Shouting names down the hall from the study as the rest of the family ate large bowls of boiled fish and johnnycake the next-door neighbour brought instead of flowers.

"The ministers and the Governor General sit on the other side of the church," Diplomat Auntie yelled with authority. "The GG in the front row."

"Please rise," the priest says now. Everyone stands as the Governor General enters. I grab the baby from Pretty Cousin and sit firmly in my seat, despite the look of admonition I receive from my mother—the Aunties. *Fat Johnny*, I think to myself. The Governor General grew up in the same neighbourhood as my mother. The lot beside Bahamas Bus and Truck. I've seen his fat brown face peeking around the front gate, out of focus in old photographs. Everyone but Diplomat Auntie still calls him Johnny.

I clutch the baby and stare straight ahead. The flowers on top of the coffin blur as my eyes fill.

Pretty Cousin is flying. Leaning far out the limousine window, camera in hand. All it would take is just one push. I am in the car behind hers, sandwiched between Small Auntie and my mother. We cannot see the picture she is taking. Later I will examine the photograph, the pallbearers walking behind the hearse. Heads soaked in sweat. My husband on the left side between Only Uncle and Spanish Cousin with one eye. One of the older men, out of focus, listing to one side with exhaustion.

There's an easy path to the graveyard. At the bottom of the cathedral stairs you turn left and cut through the parking lot, the basketball court. But my family wants the cortege to drive my grandmother—who never learned to swim—past the ocean. We have a police escort. Diplomat Auntie arranged it. A young policeman in his dress whites and bobby-style hat stops traffic with a gloved hand. Our procession inches down West Hill Street onto Bay Street and up Nassau Street. Past the crowded jitneys, the tourists on scooters, past the tennis courts at the British Colonial, a vacant lot where one worker is eating his lunch, and the new Holiday Inn Junkanoo. Cicadas scream outside the window as the heat rises.

Inside our limousine my mother and Small Auntie lean across me in a huddle. "Mrs. Rolle, Mr. Sim and his daughter, Mrs. Clark." My mother counts on her long fingers as Small Auntie jots names down on a piece of paper. They are calculating the mourner-to-food ratio. As they speak, tents are being erected in the backyard of my grandmother's house. The caterer setting a neat row of chafing dishes on a table. A bar stationed under the pear tree where Diplomat Auntie has hung her prized purple orchid. A cluster of round tables covered in starched white linens that will soften in the midday heat. The Birds of Paradise in bloom. A brilliant red and yellow stain in the thick green. A backyard scene that will look much like the rehearsal dinner the night before my husband and I married. The same crowd, only this time in black and white.

"Three pans of stuffed crabs, two plates of egg salad sandwiches, fruit salad," says Small Auntie, leaning across my lap with her pad of paper.

"There are more people than at your wedding," my mother says, more to Small Auntie than to me.

"That reminds me. Let's use those bowls from her rehearsal dinner," my mother says.

"Yes, yes," agrees Small Auntie, placing her cell phone in my hand. "Call the house and tell them to get those out of the back room." She pulls her mantilla across her cheek as someone walks by the car.

I ignore her, stare at the phone, shuffle my shoes on the floor of the limousine like an angry child. Look at the beach sand crushed into the carpet. The smell of stale brine in the seat cushions.

We arrive at the graveyard, never having looked at the ocean.

St. Francis of Assisi Cemetery has no grand entrance, no polished gates that whine politely when opened. There are no royal palms rustling a mournful shush, no attentive caretakers to remove long-dead flowers. A simple graveyard in the middle of the city, sandwiched between hotels, beachfront daiquiri stands and the main road. The Aunties would have chosen a more significant graveyard if there were one. But this is the best kept of Catholic graveyards.

Today the graveyard is tidy. Grass clipped to a polite length, weeds pulled. Workmen opened my grandfather's vault, chipped his coffin out from beneath the concrete slab and cut the coral rock to push it down further. Making room for my grandmother's grander coffin. Tall Auntie paid for it. And all the extra expenses. The tent in the corner of the graveyard, the large sisal rug carpeting the grass, slipcovered chairs facing the open crypt. There aren't enough seats for everyone. Groups gather away from the event under casuarina trees for what little shade they offer. Old friends stand in the direct sun like a penance. *Click, click.* Pretty Cousin takes one last shot over my shoulder before we enter the graveyard. Oldest Auntie has the baby now. Still groggy, the baby can barely hold her head up to drink from her pink cup. Oldest Auntie pulls her mantilla over the baby's face. I want to pass the baby to the Umbrella Man, the government official with a black and white parasol who walks a step behind Diplomat Auntie, steadying her by the elbow with his free hand. She walks in a small halo of shade as the midday sun bleaches the limestone walls and headstones a brilliant white.

We walk through the iron gates behind the coffin, down the grass pathway toward the tent. The path is too narrow. Barely contains the coffin and eight pallbearers. The men on the left side step on the edges of other graves. "We should have measured the width," my mother's eyes say as she darts a look back at me. She brought a measuring tape when we visited the site last night. I grabbed it away when the family of the man in the next plot arrived. My grandmother's soon-to-be neighbour, whose burial slab we carpet, set chairs upon. We approximated the size of the coffin, the width of the men. Accounted for their different heights. I raise my head now and see—as my mother predicted—my husband, the tallest, struggling with the most weight.

There is a Rastafarian who sings after the prayers, a man who sells fruit outside Diplomat Auntie's office. It startles me when he starts to sing. I think he has wandered in off Nassau street. A construction worker. An interloper. He stands apart under a nearby tree in his T-shirt and worn jeans, oiled dreadlocks partially contained in a colourful knit cap. His voice has a rough beauty. A throat-clearing sound. *Lead me, guide me along the way, for You lead me, I cannot stray.*

People fan themselves with funeral programs. The crowd disperses. People moving back to their cars for air conditioning.

The casket has been lowered into the ground. Final prayers said. But we don't leave. "We want to make sure they do it right," Tall Auntie says, motioning to the Haitian workers crouched on the sidewall, waiting with buckets and trowels. The men work quickly. *Yes, miss. Yes, miss.* Move the concrete slab on top of my grandmother's coffin and reseal the edges with mortar. My family stands and watches. *Click, click.* "Smooth that edge," Tall Auntie says, as if supervising a home renovation. "A little more." She grabs the trowel in frustration. Hiking up her skirt, bends down and scoops more mortar out of the bucket, slops it in a wet pile in the corner of the slab. "Like this."

Small Auntie rolls her eyes. And my mother says, "For God's sake, people are watching." Tall Auntie continues. Takes off her suit jacket and throws it on a nearby chair.

The Haitians' eyes widen. "Miss lady, miss lady," they say, circling the grave. "I do it, please, please." But she keeps working, doesn't even raise her head. Her mantilla falls into her eyes and she bats it away with a free hand.

"If. You. Want. Things. Done. Right," she barks out with puffs of exertion. Sweat is dripping down her arm. Antiperspirant leaves a chalky residue on her tailor-made dress. Pretty Cousin stands frozen for a moment. *Click, click.* Tall Auntie stops. Hefts a leg on to the edge of the grave and sits on her haunches to examine her work.

She wordlessly passes the trowel to the closest Haitian, who helps her up, repeating *Thankyoumiss, thankyoumiss* in an endless loop.

We pass the baby back and forth with both care and indifference, like a bag of easily broken groceries. She is awake now and the front of her dress is drenched. Her little body generating so much heat. It's my turn to hold her. I stand with her in the sun at the foot of the grave. Watch as the Aunties supervise the arrangement of flowers on the still-wet concrete. The Haitians move quickly. Responding instantaneously to the barrage of orders. Small Auntie moves in and places a wreath in the middle with a banner draped across it that reads *España* in gold glitter. An offering I assume is from my grandmother's family in Spain. Their countrywoman buried in the same stone as Spanish pirates and sailors who also dared to cross the ocean.

There is a pewter plaque with her name on it inside the coffin. Tall Auntie insisted. She read a hurricane story from the Out Islands about graveyards washed out to sea. Flooded cemeteries giving up their dead. Coffins bobbing in the ocean. Some caught in the branches of trees as the water subsided. Experts needed to identify the remains.

"*Goyita.*" I whisper her name as I tuck the baby under the brim of my hat. A cool feeling seems to pass over me when they are done with the flowers. When she is securely in the ground. I think it is a cloud, maybe a storm rolling in.

Only later will I see the parasol in the picture Pretty Cousin snaps. The lens flares the sunlight above us, washing the sky like a ghost. And the Umbrella Man who holds it over us. He is tall with round eyeglasses. A bald statue with a neatly trimmed moustache, creating a perfect circle of shade for the baby and me.

But standing there, I believe it is a cloud. An answer to my prayers in church—my singular plea was for rain—a blanket of heavy clouds to protect my grandmother from the spotlight.

This picture is out of place. A big woman in small spandex shorts and a pink tank top watches the funeral from the wall. A silver camera looped around her right wrist, a beach bag over her left shoulder. She has wandered away from Bay Street. In search of the *real* Nassau. A dilapidated pink or yellow house, naked babies in front yards, old black people in chairs on front porches. I look at her and want to hiss, want to walk over to the gate and swat her with my free arm between the bars. I think I see a glint off her camera lens, but I tell myself it is the sun bouncing off a passing car mirror. My eyes playing tricks on me through the Woman's Tongue tree that grows up the wall in the corner of the graveyard. Its trunk pressed against the wall, as though trying not to intrude. The branches grow in one direction, casting a long shadow over the grave. And its dried pods rustle together in a whisper about the passing years. I know this tree from old photographs I found three days ago while helping Tall Auntie find a picture for the funeral program. What should have been a simple program, the usual eulogy, order of service and hymns, produced with the attention to detail of an annual report. Last minute rewording, a meeting at the mahogany dining-room table where colours and paper stock and font were discussed. The picture of my grandmother that I chose was taken at my wedding. A magenta dress, a white orchid with flushed pink edges pinned to her lapel. The colour won't be as true in the program. The paper quality cheaper than Tall Auntie requested, the printer's error despite the phone calls to check on the progress of the piece. "We have explicitly asked for 24-bond, if the printer cannot accommodate this you must contact us before you proceed," Tall Auntie said slowly and deliberately into the receiver.

She nodded to Diplomat Auntie, who yelled, "Tell them they must bring it directly here, not to the church. We need to see it done."

Over the wall the tourist crosses herself and raises her camera. *Click, click.* One funeral photo in a roll of beach shots.

I lower the brim of my hat so I can no longer see her. I bow my head and pretend that this is a normal funeral where faces and the position of bodies are not recorded, where memory will be allowed to blur the edges and distort the colours. Later, I will look at the overexposed pictures, the angle of faces, the backs of hats, and still catch a whiff of spicy Opium perfume mixed with musk. The smell of Nassau dressed for a funeral.

The last image is from the beginning. Me at the funeral home, touching my grandmother when no one is looking. Pressing my forehead, my lips into the cotton of her blue dress. It smells bittersweet with old talcum powder. It smells like everything I have missed three thousand miles away.

There is no picture of this.

ACKNOWLEDGEMENTS

I am grateful for the financial assistance of the Canada Council for the Arts and the Alberta Foundation for the Arts. These grants were instrumental in the successful completion of this collection.

For her sharp eye and tireless enthusiasm for students, past and present, I thank Aritha van Herk; for their skilled assistance and constant support, I am grateful to my classmates at the University of Calgary, most affectionately, Gisèle Villeneuve, Adrian Kelly, Anne Sorbie, Samuel Pane, & Athene Evans; for her flawless insight and loving friendship, I thank Marika Deliyannides.

I owe many thanks to generous writers who have encouraged me along the way, especially Rosemary Nixon, Dave Margoshes and David Carpenter.

For emotional support, I thank my friends outside the writing community, especially Teresa Scarlett and my sister, Nadia Honnet, for their unwavering belief in me.

I wish to offer my heartfelt thanks to my publisher, Turnstone Press, especially Wayne Tefs and Todd Besant; to my ever-generous family in Canada and the Bahamas, for being more excited than I could ever could have imagined at having a writer in the family, especially my father, David Honnet, who has patiently read and pondered all these stories.

Finally, my deepest gratitude and love to my husband, Aaron Hilger, and our son Oliver for making my life outside these pages so joyful.

The following stories first appeared as follows:

"Conversion Classes" in *The Journey Prize Stories 15* and *filling Station*, "Limbo" in *Event* magazine, "How to Raise a Smart Baby" in *PRISM international*, and "Famished" in *Room of One's Own*.

In "How to Raise a Smart Baby" there are excerpts from *Brain Power: Working out the human mind* by Professor Susan Greenfield (Element Books Ltd., 1999).

In "Conversion Classes" the marriage preparation questions are from *For Better & For Ever: Sponsor Couple Program for Christian Marriage Preparation (Roman Catholic Edition)* by Robert A. Ruhnky, CSSR (Liguori Publications, 1981).

In "The Pepper Smuggler" the legend of Draupadi is paraphrased from http:/cs.art.rmit.edu.au/projects/media/elephants/draupadi/story/legend.html and instructions for draping a sari are from www.indianwomenonline.com.